Sanchita Karma

and Other Tales of Ethics
and Choice from India

By K. V. Dominic

Foreword by Dr. Ramesh K. Srivastava

Modern History Press
Ann Arbor, MI

Sanchita Karma and Other Tales of Ethics and Choice from India
Copyright © 2018 by K.V. Dominic. All Rights Reserved
Learn more at www.ProfKVDominic.com

Library of Congress Cataloging-in-Publication Data

Names: Dominic, K. V. (Kannappillil Varghese), 1956- author.
Title: Sanchita Karma and other tales of ethics and choice from India / by K. V. Dominic.
Description: Ann Arbor, MI : Modern History Press, 2018. | Includes index.
Identifiers: LCCN 2018020154 (print) | LCCN 2018032113 (ebook) | ISBN 9781615993956 (Kindle, ePub, pdf) | ISBN 9781615993932 (pbk. : alk. paper) | ISBN 9781615993949 (hardcover : alk. paper)
Classification: LCC PR9499.4.D66 (ebook) | LCC PR9499.4.D66 A6 2018 (print) |
    DDC 823/.92--dc23
LC record available at https://lccn.loc.gov/2018020154

Published by
Modern History Press
5145 Pontiac Trail
Ann Arbor, MI 48105

www.ModernHistoryPress.com
info@ModernHistoryPress.com

Tollfree 888-761-6268 (USA/Can)
Fax 734-663-6861

Distributed by Ingram (USA/CAN/AU), Betram's Books (UK/EU)

Cover Photo: provided by Goa Outreach Project

Dedicated to
My dear wife Anne, Daughter Rose Ann,
&
Son Joe George

Contents

Foreword

A creative writer is a sensitive being whose imagination gets stirred even by minor vibrations from within or without, but is jolted into action when the wellbeing of a large section of society is at stake. Prof. K. V. Dominic's poems and short stories are the concretization of these creative impulses. While his annoyance over minor social problems finds spontaneous articulation in his poems, major universal issues such as corruption and bribery, superstition, political and religious exploitation, unemployment and underemployment, exploitation of nature and animals, among other things, find elaborate expression in his short stories.

Kerala has the highest literacy rate in the country and its biggest problem is the unemployment and underemployment of educated youth. The problem has been highlighted in three short stories: "Who is Responsible?" "The Best Government Servant," and "Twisted Course of Destiny." Anwar, in the first story, has to work in Oman, leaving behind his ailing parents and newly-married bride at home. As a result of his absence from home, a litany of tragedy ensues. Krishnan, in the second story, though underemployed, refuses to accept the widely-prevalent practice of taking bribes and is transferred to a remote place. He takes the high road and his temerity leads to a surprising solution. In "Twisted Course of Destiny," Rajiv with M.Sc. and Ph.D. degrees gets a peon's job and has to work under much less qualified senior colleagues.

Religious and political exploitation, along with the evils of superstition, find good representation in some of his stories. "Burn Your Horoscope" is a powerful story highlighting gullible and credulous persons who remain closed-minded against logic. It takes many years to counter such a toxic prophecy. In "Joseph's Maiden Vote for Parliament," the protagonist refuses to vote when he finds all the candidates undesirable and corrupt. "Matthews, the Real Christian" depicts the tragic death of a person who was Christian in words and deeds.

The writer's concern for nature and animals finds expression in three stories, which are reminiscent of Vishnu Sarma's *Panchatantra* and Rudyard Kipling's *Jungle Book*. They are really close cousins of fables and tales, in which various animals and objects of nature communicate with one another as would human beings. In the same tradition, Krishnan and Stephen in "Sanchita Karma" have respectively been painted all white and all black. While the former is a lover of birds, animals and plants, the latter hates them and as such kills seven cats.

Due to his past accumulated deeds, he has to be reborn as mouse in the next life. The two kittens in "The Twins" are contrasted with human beings. They remain clean and give pleasure to all the members of the family. In "World Environment Day," Katturaja is a modified and transformed version of the notorious gangster Veerappan who roamed all over the forest, killing tuskers and cutting sandalwood trees. Under the influence of nature, Katturaja is so much transformed that he becomes a great preserver of nature.

A very thin line divides pure literature and literature-with-a-purpose, and that line has become nearly invisible in these stories. This is due largely to the writer's intensely-felt anguish over social ills as also due to his overwhelming concern to rectify these social distortions by giving them an overtly-visible representation. K. V. Dominic's *Sanchita Karma and Other Tales of Ethics and Choice from India* is undoubtedly a laudable effort in making these stories a powerful instrument for eradication of prevalent evils in the country.

Dr. Ramesh K. Srivastava
Novelist & critic, former Professor of English,
Guru Nanak Dev University, Amritsar, Punjab, India

Preface

With immense happiness I present before my esteemed readers this second collection of my short stories. The twenty stories in this book have been written over a period of ten years. My first short story, "The Twins," was composed in 2008 and the last, "I am Unwanted," just a week ago. It was much easier for me to find themes for my poems, while an outline for a story came to my mind once in a blue moon. Being a social critic, I can easily vent my anger and emotion over social evils and issues instantly through poetry.

Almost all the stories in the collection have been published through my own edited journals, as well as through international journals, both print and online. The story "Who is Responsible?" won great acclaim and appreciation when it was published in the online journal *Muse India* (issue 30, March-April 2010). It was the leading story of a number of stories called for and selected by the special story editor. In my stories, I have used several themes and focussed on many issues which are universal and at the same time frequently occurring in my own State, Kerala.

The themes include loneliness and the problems of old age, thirst for love, sexual desires, robbery and murder, terrorism, humanism and compassion, corruption and bribery in government offices, honesty and duty consciousness, fair judgement, cruel destiny, superstitions and exploitations in the name of religion, fight against superstitions, politics and political exploitation, Christian spirit versus Christian practice, miseries of the poor and the marginalised, indifference and cruelty to the poor, cruelty to animals and punishment for it, problems of the educational system, problems of unemployment, beauty of the natural world, love and compassion to animals, exploitation of forests, conversion and conservation, religious fanaticism and multicultural harmony, the impact of the mother tongue in education, sexism and women empowerment etc.

I wish all my esteemed readers an interesting and enlightening voyage through my book!

Dr. K. V. Dominic

1 – The Twins

"Why do you let that cat into our kitchen? It will eat our food when you are away," I told my wife who was battling in the kitchen in the early hours of the morning.

"You are busy with your computer upstairs, and who is there with me to save me from my loneliness? So I have invited Sundari into the kitchen," my wife replied.

Sundari, the name my wife had given to that stray cat, was left out by our nearest neighbours who shifted to another place. Sundari was not that *sundari* (beautiful), but an average cat of native breed with pink and white colours. Being a stray cat, it was frightened when I or my son approached. None of us was allowed to stroke her, but the very touch and cry of the cat removed my wife's solitude.

In a way I am guilty of leaving my wife alone in the kitchen for too many hours. She is not a feminist and so she never insisted that I should help her in cooking. We belong to a patriarchal family line, and the men in the family have superiority over women. So my wife was never demanding, but I should have helped her instead of sending emails to my friends. She didn't want the help of a servant, fearing the loss of privacy. When I teach feminism to my students, I pray to God to dissuade the students from asking its practice in my own life. A teacher should be a model to the students.

My wife's friendship with Sundari continued and the bond became stronger and stronger. Still she could not stroke the cat. Sundari became pregnant and after one or two months it gave birth to two kittens, both photocopies of the mother. They were brought down to the kitchen from the berth after a week. Now my wife had three companions in place of one. Her kitchen work became smoother and happier. I was also entertained by the plays of the kittens. Then one of the kittens was found missing. What happened to it is still unknown. Since my wife was happy with the cats, I decided to buy a beautiful kitten of foreign pedigree, which we could stroke, have on our lap, and have communication with it. When I expressed my desire, one of my colleagues told me that he would supply me a twin instead of one. Accordingly, I went to his house and he presented me a carton bearing the twins. The carton was opened in one of our rooms after shutting its door. My wife and my son were very anxious to look at the guests. Two angels got out of the carton. Indeed, they were very, very beautiful. They had snowy white fur except for dark spots on their head and tails. The tails were thick and bushy, characteristic of the Ooty cats. Pairs of emeralds on their heads looked at us. The twins were not scared at all. My wife placed some milk before them and they drank a little. Then they started their running. They were identical twins; one had more dark spots on the head than the other. My wife named them Manikutty and Amminikutty.

Needless to say, these twins brought our innocent childhood back. We started to behave like children ourselves, playing with these twins. Sundari and its kitten were ignored. In fact, they refused to come to the kitchen as the twins encroached on the place. Still, food was supplied to them in the backyard.

A plastic ball was bought for the twins. The way they played football was more thrilling than watching the World Cup. Naturally the agility of these kittens is superior to the World Cup heroes.

Along with pleasures, the twins supplied us burdens and restrictions. For the first three days, they used our bedroom, particularly the bed and pillows, as their toilet. We had to wash the sheets, replace pillows and even change the entire bed. As a precaution, the bedrooms and the reading room had to be kept shut, always. The beautiful sofa cover was pulled down by the twins who promptly urinated on it. The sofa thus remained without its cover and it became the place for sharpening their nails.

Still, these problems and hardships had a sweetness, albeit a bitter sweetness! Gradually, the twins started to use the bathrooms instead of the closets for their waste. It was my duty to remove the excrement and sterilize the bathroom. It had to be done thrice a day. The twins, when not playing, wanted to sit on our laps. The very jump on to the lap when we were reading or writing pricked our thighs with their tiny claws. Once, when my leg started to bleed, I was worried. I had read that the nail wounds from cats could cause rabies. As the twins were not affected by rabies, I risked not taking anti-rabies injections myself.

Manikutty demanded more strokes and care from us than Amminikutty. She, not satisfied with our strokes, would climb on a shoulder and even on to the head. Although they don't bathe with water and soap as we do twice a day, how clean are their bodies! But how many times they do bathe their bodies with their saliva? We have to learn much from Nature.

Their clutches with the nails pained me and I had to wear a shirt always to save my chest, especially nipples.

Remember, the kittens had been fed by their mother when I brought them. On the third day of their arrival, as I was reading a newspaper in the morning, the twins jumped on to my lap and started crying. I stroked them, but it couldn't pacify them. "What are they crying for? They have been fed just now. Have gone to the toilet? Yes, that's also done. Then what?" I thought.

Why didn't God give speech power to non-human beings? In a way it's better they don't have it. The sound pollution than man makes is deadlier than atomic radiation! The nasty, ugly words that dart from his mouth can annihilate millions! In fact it boomerangs to the Creator Himself! Man plays a discordant note to the symphony which all other creatures make in this universe. "Miau, miau, miau, miau," the twins were still pestering me. "What do you want? What are you crying for?" I asked. "Maa, maa, maa, maa," the tone was different. "Oh! They are calling for their mother," I could read their language. Probably they were asking me where their mother was.

An arrow pierced through my heart. I'd never thought of their attachment to their mother. I could read also their mother's moans. Was it not cruel of me to snatch away these little ones from their mother? The thought pricked me and my heart started to bleed. Shall I return the twins to their mother? No, I shouldn't be so sentimental. After all, life is a sum of innumerable meetings and partings! God has given His creations the strength to bear such pangs! I sought refuge in such philosophies.

There are many things we human beings can learn from these 'sub-human' beings. (Are we superior to them except in brain and speech?) The expression of these twins' love—their kissing each other, hugs, licking one another, sleeping on one other's body, eating and drinking from the same plate, playing together etc. etc.—were real feasts for our eyes and mind. They were the real beauties! When they were around me I couldn't pluck my eyes from them. Indeed they were joys forever! Their dangling on the door curtains, climbing over the grills, sitting together on the TV, dining table, especially on the newspaper, like two marble statues—were treats for us!

Once, Amminikutty climbed over a window through its curtain and started dangling on the flicker lamp at the foot of my father's photograph. Had my father been alive in the photo, he would have picked the kitten and hugged it, for he was a lover of cats when he lived. In my childhood we reared a cat always to kill the mice. The cats used to sleep with us.

The twins' play went to such an extreme that they climbed on a tender chilli plant my wife nursed with extra care in the backyard. My wife used to pluck hot chillies from it. The plant was completely wrecked. Instead of anger, we felt only happiness. Had the mischief been done by my son when he was a child, we would have punished him, because God has given him reasoning power. Human beings, having developed brains, do all sorts of crimes and evils other animals never do.

One day, as I was having tea in the College canteen, one of my colleagues read the news about five murders committed by a man. He killed his wife, hid the body in the septic tank; two days later he raped his own little daughter, killed her and her brother and buried them somewhere; after three days he brought his remaining two children from the school, killed them and locked the bodies in a room.

Commenting on this diabolical act, one teacher said, "How can one become so brutal?"

I told him rather hotly, "Dear friend, don't dishonour animals with such speech. Never compare such human activities to animals.' Does any animal attack another without any reason? Except for food, do animals kill other creatures? Do they attack us unless they are provoked, disturbed or scared? The very term "brutal" has to be redefined." All the teachers assembled there agreed to my views.

Eventually, things went very smoothly in our house. The twins made our house a heaven. Our daughter in New Delhi eagerly waited for the holidays after six months to experience the twins' play. She intended to bring toys for them. As her birthday was approaching I wrote this story for her as this year's birthday gift.

A few days later my wife told me, "Dear, what will our mother do when she comes here to stay tomorrow? How can she manage the twins when we leave her alone from ten to four on working days?" Our mother was eighty-seven years old, weak, and a heart patient. She was prolonging her life by taking countless tablets. She'd been staying in my brother's house for a few months, and wishe to stay with us for some months. How could I tell her not to come to our house since we have two kittens?

I told my wife, "Don't worry, dear, mother will manage. Or, shall we give back the kittens to the teacher who gave them to us?" Though I asked her this, I never intended to do it.

"No question of leaving these angels," my wife replied.

"OK, we will manage the crisis somehow," I told her.

My mother was brought to our house the next day. She was delighted to see those kittens. She enjoyed their playful antics. The next day, Monday, my wife had to go to her school and, I to my college. Leaving mother's food and medicines on the table in her room for her intake at noon, I went to work. The twins were fed and they were sleeping then. Extra food was placed for them in the kitchen. I prayed to God that the twins should not create any problem for my mother.

At one o' clock I returned home for my lunch. When I opened the front door I could hear the gasping sound of my mother. I rushed to her bedroom and found that she was struggling for breath. I asked if she took the medicine. She replied in a very low voice, "The kittens scattered the tablets on the floor while I was sleeping." True, I found the scattered white tablets on the white-tiled floor, which she could not herself make out. The food was also scattered on the floor.

At once I gave her emergency medicine to ensure her easy breathing. I cleaned the floor. The twins were found sleeping on the dining table. I started to think, "Who is dearer to me, mother or the kittens? No doubt my mother, who gave me birth and nurtured me to this position." Though reluctantly, I took the carton in which the twins were brought, put the sleeping kittens in it and tied with twine. Mother was gradually recovering. I told her, "Ma, I have to go to college now. You will be OK after a few minutes. I shall return after one hour."

"OK, you may go," mother replied.

I took the carton to my car, and drove along the road. Beyond the town I reached a lonely area. I stopped the car. The twins were still sleeping. My heart started to tighten. I felt a kind of suffocation in my throat. It was very painful for me to part with the cats. *Am I doing right or wrong? If they were to be disposed so, why did I bring them to my house? Wouldn't they have lived happily in my colleague's house?* A series of wounding questions strangled my heart. I had to make a decision. Gathering all my energy, I took the carton and placed it on the side of the road.

With shaking hands I opened it. The kittens were awakening. They were startled by the new surroundings. Weeping, I bade them goodbye. I got into the car and started the engine. The twins came to the door of the car, crying. Weren't they asking me, "Pappa, are you leaving us? Please don't leave us. Please don't leave us. How will we live? Who will feed us? Wouldn't it better for you to kill us?" I broke into tears.

Suddenly my cellphone rang. It was my mother. *God! Is she seriously ill?* "Ma, what happened?" I asked.

"Where are the kittens? I can't find them in the house!"

"Ma, I have left them on the road since they are trouble to us," I said.

"Are you mad? What wrong have they done? They have reasoning power as we do have! Bring them back," she cried.

"But ma..." I whispered.

"No but. If you can't, then you may discard me also!"

"OK, ma. I am bringing them back," I consoled her. Life was restored to me. My breathing became normal. The suffocation and the aching of the heart disappeared. I got down from the car, took the twins, hugged them, kissed them and brought them back to my house. My mother was happy again that she got back her companions. She had experienced so much solitude in my house that these kittens proved real companions to her.

"My dear son, I can't live without these angels," she said.

"Alright mother, I am going to appoint a home nurse for you and the kittens," I replied.

When my wife returned in the evening I told her what had happened. She was horrified to hear of my cruelty to the twins. She too agreed to appoint a home nurse. Until we get one, I decided to take several short leaves of absence. Thus our house became heaven again!

~ ~ ~

2 – World Environment Day

Kaatturaja is the most notorious forest thief in Karnataka, India. As his name suggests, he is the king of the forest. Six foot tall, a sturdy youth of thirty, he is ebony black with a twisted moustache on his ferocious face. In addition to thousands of costly trees he has stolen, he has hunted many wild animals and even elephants for their tusks. The State government has offered one million rupees for information leading to his capture. He has ambushed forest rangers several times, but fortunately none was killed.

Kaatturaja is the illegitimate son of a tribal woman named Kanni. At the age of sixteen when Kanni was collecting firewood in the forest, two forest rangers raped her. Although she reported the matter to her parents, they were not courageous enough to complain to the police station, which was several kilometres away from their hut. Moreover, it was a futile attempt to complain since tribal people's wails were never heeded by the government.

Illiterate Kanni gave birth to a son and he lived among other tribal children of the forest as a bastard. Kanni was married to a youth when Kaatturaja was only two years old. Thus Kaatturaja lived with his grandparents, despised by all except his mother. Occasionally, his mother visited him and presented him sweets, and the delicacies he liked the most.

Kaatturaja grew up from teenager to young adult, fed by anger and a wish for revenge against the establishment and the world that had discarded him as an outcast. The tribal people lived in a very miserable condition. They didn't get any financial assistance from the government, even though tens of millions of rupees were allotted to them. These monies were misappropriated and looted by the government officials. There were no hospitals, schools or even good roads for them. They survived on what Nature fed them through the forest—tubers, honey, fish from brooks, meat of small animals like rat, rabbit, wild boar etc.

Kaatturaja was sent to a school in the nearby village and got a primary education, which opened his eyes. He learnt how his people were exploited by the government and forest mafia. On becoming a young man, he decided to help his people by working as a forest thief. He was helped by his friends there and started cutting costly trees of the forest—teak, sandalwood, rosewood, mahogany, and the like, and sold them to agents of timber merchants. They did it in the thick of the forest where forest rangers seldom patrolled. The money they earned was distributed to the poor families for various purposes such as purchasing dresses from the town, getting treatment for the sick. Kaatturaja never felt any guilt for his illegal acts, but took it as a sweet revenge on the government.

On World Environment Day, June 5th 2011, Kaatturaja was all alone in the forest and was trying to fell a teak tree. Being their own holiday, the forest and its inhabitants were celebrating. A gentle breeze kissed and stroked all trees, birds and animals. One could sense the mirth of Nature from the chirping of birds, laughing of leaves, mating calls and other happy cries of animals. The teak sensed the advent of its death and cried for help. Insensible to human beings, the cry reached the ears of elephants grazing on a mound nearby.

"Isn't that an alarm cry of a tree?" the tusker asked the cow elephants.

"True. We won't allow any human being to trespass our dwelling place this special day," the other elephants replied.

"Let's charge them then," the tusker said.

Kaatturaja lifted his axe to cut, and the roaring elephants rushed at him. Frightened, he shot up the tree like a rocket. The elephants stood beneath the tree, waiting for his descent. The teak tree thanked the elephants through its rustling applause of leaves. Kaatturaja, who had never been timid in his youth, started shivering.

It seemed that the tree was talking to him: "Dear friend, what harm have I done to you that you should kill me? See how I became your saviour just now! What harm have this forest and its animals done to you? Haven't you felled thousands of trees and hunted hundreds of animals? You and your people survive only because of our presence. Who cuts the branch he sits upon? If you continue to destroy this forest, how and where will those elephants and other animals live?"

"I am sorry dear tree. Kindly forgive me," Kaatturaja started weeping with clasped palms. He then spoke in a loud voice to the entire forest: "In the name of this forest I promise you all that I will trouble you no more. Please pardon me for the crimes I have done. I will be your friend from this very moment and devote my life to the preservation of this forest." His voice echoed in the forest and his conversion was welcomed by the entire forest with cheers. The trees swayed and danced. Birds twittered. Animals cried in joy. The elephants standing below went away, swinging their trunks in happiness.

With a sigh of relief, Kaatturaja climbed down the tree and thanked it once again for saving his life. He went to his house, changed his clothes and went straight to the magistrate's office in the nearby town. He got permission to get into the magistrate's room.

He told the magistrate, "Honourable sir, I am Kaatturaja, the sought-after forest thief. I have come to surrender. I would like to do penance for the crimes I have committed. You may arrest me."

The magistrate gave orders for his arrest. He told him, "It's a great thing that you have surrendered. You will be jailed now and there will be a trial. You can tell the court whatever you want at that time."

Kaatturaja was sent to the district jail. As part of the investigation, he was taken by the police to the forest several times. He admitted all charges against him and pointed out the places where he'd felled the trees. After a month, he was brought to the court for the trial. The public prosecutor pleaded for the government and presented the crimes Kaatturaja had committed. Kaatturaja had no advocates to defend him and he accepted all the charges presented by the public prosecutor. The judge then asked Kaatturaja if he had anything to state or plead before the court.

Kaatturaja replied, "You honour, it is true that I have committed unpardonable crimes and did a lot of damage to the forest. I now sincerely feel that I should not have been so hostile to the forest and the environment. I should have abided by the laws of the government and supported it in its activities for the welfare of the people and nature. You may punish me. But if the government is merciful enough, I can devote the rest of my life to the conservation and preservation of the forest I have destroyed. The court may kindly believe my words that I will no more break the laws of the government, but will support to the best of my ability all welfare projects. If you allow me, I will make a taskforce in the forest with my friends, and along with them volunteer for the preservation and conservation of the forest. We will not allow any intruders to exploit the forest anymore. As a penance for the crimes I have done, we will plant thousands of trees in the forest and thus make it the best forest in the world."

The judge replied, "The court is happy to hear such good words from you. Accepting your promise, the court is giving you a light punishment for the innumerable crimes you have committed. You are going to be imprisoned for one year, and it is test dose as to see if your conversion is genuine or not. If you prove your goodness of heart, you will be released and then as you promised you can make the taskforce and serve the forest."

Kaatturaja was imprisoned in the district jail and he was a model prisoner, favourite of the jail authorities as well as the fellow prisoners. He thus showed that he had become a purified and sanctified being.

5th June 2012. World Environment Day. The court released Kaatturaja and allowed him to go back to the forest. The forest welcomed sanctified Kaatturaja with clapping leaves. The gentle breeze stroked him. Birds sang his welcome music. Monkeys chattered and led him to the midst of the forest. Elephants grazing in the meadow sensed his arrival and trumpeted. It was a grand homecoming for Kaatturaja. The forest accepted him as its saviour Raja.

As pledged and promised, Kaatturaja made a taskforce with his friends. The team of energetic twenty-odd youth started reforestation wherever barren strips were found. The forest rangers had little to do at all since Kaatturaja's team never allowed any trespassers to steal from the forest. After two years, the forest became a model to the world and the country nominated Kaatturaja and his team for the United Nations Forest for People Award.

~ ~ ~

3 – Is Human Life More Precious than an Animal's?

Prof. Antony Francis is shocked by the video clip of the 9 pm news on the Asianet News Channel. A cow is trying to jump out of the pen of a moving truck overloaded with cattle. The street is thronged with innumerable vehicles flowing like a river. The cattle truck is coming from Tamil Nadu to Kerala. Hundreds of such trucks carrying cattle from Tamil Nadu and Andhra Pradesh are rushing to the butcher houses in Kerala every day. The cattle traders pack the trucks with more cattle than permitted by bribing the road transport authorities. Poor animals, they suffer horribly, not able to stand well, or when tired, unable to rest by lying.

The cow might have sensed the danger that she was being carried for slaughter; or unable to stand in the same posture anymore, she decided to get out of hell. After a few attempts, she succeeded in jumping down. The cattle trader or the owner of the cow sitting beside the driver noted it through the mirror of the truck and got down immediately. The cow was running between the speeding vehicles, followed by the owner.

The cow crossed the divider of the street and ran across the opposite lane. The owner followed it a in panic. A truck struck the cow and she fell down with a loud scream, limbs trembling violently. She died instantly. The vehicles stopped. The owner was weeping, not because of any sympathy for the animal, but because of the monetary loss due to its death. The video reporter too expressed no sympathy to the cow or sadness at her death. He commented that had the cow not been killed or just crossed the road safely, a man would have lost his life because the truck would have hit him instead. His tone was that of a relief at the man's life saved.

Prof. Antony's wife Teresa was also viewing the TV, and she shared same view of the video reporter. "God saved the cattle dealer. Only the cow was killed. Even otherwise it would be butchered within a couple of days," Teresa commented. Teresa is Associate Professor of English in St. Anne's Women's College, a government aided college run by the Christian management in the town. Prof. Antony is Professor of Zoology in the Government College in the same town.

"Teresa, you have no grief for the cow, it seems. My heart is aching at her tragic death. I don't feel any sympathy for the owner. He is responsible for the death of the cow. He is a murderer."

"Why should we feel so much sympathy for an animal? God has created animals for man's use and comfort. Similarly, all other creations in the universe. Isn't man the centre of all creation? Aren't we the children of God, who created us in His image?"

"Rubbish. Who told you that Man is the centre of all creation? Or that God created Man in his image?"

"Why, the Bible says so. Haven't you studied it? Only we human beings have souls and hence the choicest of all God's creations, and thus the children of God."

"There lies the problem. I believe and my common sense tells me that to the Creator, all creations are equally good. There is nothing ugly in His creations and He loves all creations—both living bodies and non-living bodies, just like a father or mother loving all his/her children irrespective of their beauty, intelligence, health, virtues or vices.

"It's only because of man's selfishness that he thinks that he is dearer to God than other beings," he continued. "It's all because of his reasoning power that he thinks in a negative way. Other beings without such reasoning power are less selfish and more virtuous than human beings. There is universal soul and individual soul. God the Creator is the universal soul or Paramatma, whose element is there in all his creations—living and nonliving—which is called *jivatma,* or individual soul. That cow which died might have been a human being in its former life. Maybe its soul is going to take a human body again for its next existence."

"I don't understand your philosophy, dear. I haven't come across such things in the Bible."

"You should read other scriptures as well. Being an Indian, you should read and absorb Indian philosophy, ethos and culture. You should read Indian epics and scriptures like Mahabharata, Ramayana, Vedas, and Upanishads. To some extent, you are following Dvaita philosophy, as Christianity is based on it. You should learn Advaita Vedanta also. Then you will understand what I say."

"When you are there as a master teacher, why should I go after these books? Since we Christians have been brought up in a tradition where animals are considered as sub-human species and created for the welfare and pleasure of human beings, we have lost fellowship and sympathy for them. Moreover we are non-vegetarians and have no respect for animals' lives."

"Now listen to me. How I am going to react to this murder of the cow? To me, all animals are my siblings just like all human beings in the world. That exactly is the reason why I am a vegetarian now. If such an accident happened to you, what would I do? I wold file a criminal case in the court. Yes, I am going to file a case against the cattle trader who murdered the cow."

"What nonsense are you talking, dear? Filing a criminal case for an unknown, insignificant dead cow? Will the court listen to your pleas?"

"Why not? Cruelty to animals is an offence and punishable in our country. There is the Prevention of Cruelty to Animals Act introduced in 1960, which was amended in 1982. Then there is another Act called Indian Animal Welfare Act passed in 2011, which recommends maximum punishment to the offenders. I will see that the cow's murderer gets maximum punishment."

"If you are so adamant, I have nothing more to say. Best wishes to your selfless efforts for mute creatures!"

Prof. Antony contacted the Asianet TV Channel and collected the details of the truck which carried the cattle. He got the truck's registration number and learnt the whereabouts of the truck, its owner and the driver from the road transport office. The owner of the truck as well as the trader of the cattle was one and the same person, the murderer of the cow. His name was Anthappan. On further investigation, Prof. Antony could learn that Anthappan had been engaged in the cattle trade for the past ten years and had been convicted many times for overloading trucks and the cattle jumping out and running over motorcycles.

Collecting all the materials needed, Prof. Antony filed a criminal case against Anthappan in the High Court of Kerala. Since he had studied law and possessed a law degree, Prof. Antony decided to plead at the court himself. His colleagues in the college pooh-poohed him when he announced his decision. But he was not dispirited, since he knew very well that there were very few animal lovers in his locality.

The trial date came. It was the 20th of April. April is the Prevention of Cruelty to Animals month. There were only very few listeners in the court hall. Anthappan, his family and a few friends besides his advocate were present. On Prof. Antony's side, there was only his wife Teresa and their daughter and son. They were eager to see how Prof. Antony performed in court. The judge was an old man with an ash-coloured beard and round spectacles who looked very serious. He asked Prof. Antony Francis to present the case.

"Your Honour, on 1st April 2016, Mr. Anthappan's truck carried an overload of cattle through the National Highway 47 and when it reached Angamaly, a cow jumped over the gate of the truck to the street, and ran across the divider to the next lane, then was hit by a truck. Meanwhile, Mr. Anthappan was chasing it. The cow died instantly. The news was broadcast through the Ansianet TV Channel in the evening. I know there is nobody to plead for the dead cow. So I have taken it as my duty to do so. The cow, coming from Tamil Nadu, served her prime life to the people there by giving them milk and dung and when she was old and no longer of use to them, they sold her to the slaughter house in Kerala.

"The trader, Mr. Anthappan, should have ascertained the safety of the cow as well as of the other cattle he has been carrying for nearly ten years now. He should have made a strong fence or barricade instead of the one he has on his truck. Again, he should have honoured and maintained the laws of animal transportation prescribed by the road transport authorities. Instead, he packed the truck with more cattle than permitted. Poor animals, they suffered horribly, not able to stand well or when tired, unable to rest by lying. It is even doubtful that he gave them any water on the journey. Exposed to unbearable heat for several hours, and with aching legs and high fatigue, they tried to escape the hellish situation. The cow jumped down and thus tried to save herself. Mr. Anthappan chased her and she had to flee for her life, which resulted in the collision with the fast moving truck. And thus the cow had a very tragic end.

"I consider it as a murder committed by Mr. Anthappan. He has done such crimes previously, and has been fined for them. I have produced documents of those cases before you, your honour. Had it been a human being in place of the murdered cow, Mr. Anthappan would have been convicted of murder. I plead to your honour that he deserves the same punishment. Your honour, is human life more precious than animals', or animals' life valueless compared to humans'? Haven't both humans and nonhumans equal claims and rights on this planet? That's all, your honour."

The Judge then asked what the defendant had to say in response to the charges put forward by Prof. Antony. Mr. Anthappan's advocate sought permission from the Judge to interrogate Prof. Antony and Anthappan. Having got permission the advocate asked Prof. Antony if he had witnessed the accident. Prof. Antony then explained that though he had not seen the accident directly, he and millions had seen the video of the accident on TV. And he had acquired the video clips directly from the Asianet Channel, which telecast it, and it had been submitted to the court and the Judge could verify the veracity of his accusation.

Mr. Anthappan also was questioned by the advocate and he couldn't but accept the fact that the truck was overloaded and it hadn't good fencing protection for the cattle and the cow jumped down and met with the accident. He pleaded for the mercy of the court and promised that in future he would abide by the law, and no such tragedies would be repeated. Prof. Antony then reminded the court that Anthappan had given such assurances to the court during earlier trials, and had repeating the same offence again and again after paying petty fines.

The interrogations having completed, the Judge pronounced the verdict: "Since a cow has been intolerably tortured and finally led to its very tragic death, Mr. Anthappan has violated the law of Indian Animal Welfare Act. His action proves to be a criminal offence. Even though he has been warned by the court several times earlier, he has not learnt any lesson or felt any repentance. Hence he deserves the maximum punishment recommended in the Act. Mr. Anthappan shall be imprisoned for three years and he has to pay a fine of Rs. 100,000 which will be utilized for the welfare of animals." Anthappan and his family and friends were shocked by this extraordinary judgment, while Prof. Antony Francis and his family returned home jubilant. Prof. Antony could hear the soul of the dead cow telling him: "I am grateful to you, brother Professor. You have avenged my death. God bless you!"

~ ~ ~

4 – The Best Government Servant

The happiest day of his life! Dr Krishnan Namboodiri, aged 38, had gained employment as Lower Division Clerk in the Taluk Office at a small town in the State of Kerala. Though the minimum educational qualification prescribed for a clerk is SSLC (10th Class) pass, Krishnan had M.A., MPhil, PhD in Gandhian Studies. He belonged to a Brahmin family which had a wealthy lineage in the past. His still-living parents, who were living with him, were bequeathed just one acre of land. Krishnan's father was a retired school teacher and he had to spend all his hard earned savings to marry off his two daughters.

On the way to the Taluk Office to join government service, Krishnan sat comfortably in a bus, and started to ruminate on his life's journey so far. The bus would take one hour to reach the destination, leaving sufficient time for him to recollect. Krishnan had a pleasant trip in life till his age of 25, when he completed his education. From there started his bitter wounding tread over a brambly path. Characteristic of the ideal Brahmins, his father was an honest man, sincere, committed and affable to the pupils, colleagues as well as neighbours. He had never lied in his life.

Krishnan's mother, a housewife, was equally noble, affable, and of service to the neighbourhood. Krishnan had first class for his SSLC and then joined the Pre-Degree Course in Newman College, Thodupuzha. His father, a Gandhian, was his role model, and Krishnan was attracted to the Gandhian thoughts and way of life even from his childhood. The great values of Ahimsa, Non-violence, truth, patriotism etc. moulded and guided his life. Krishnan's ambition was to take PhD in Gandhian philosophy. After his Pre-Degree course, which again he passed with a first class, he enrolled in Newman College for a B.A. in History.

He was attracted to the students' union SFI (Students Federation of India), which fought for the rights of students. He was a good orator and his basic good qualities and values enabled him to become the chairman of the college union. Though SFI was leftist-oriented, Krishnan was all against violence and unnecessary strikes in the college. He graduated with a high first class, and got admission for MA in Gandhian Studies in the school of Gandhian Thought and Development Studies in Mahatma

Gandhi University, Kottayam. His scholarship was sufficient to live on, and a financial relief to his father. Krishnan was very brilliant in his studies and his teachers' favourite. After his MA, he enrolled for MPhil there, and after that, a PhD. His academic life of six years in the university campus remains the most memorable period of his life.

After his heavenly campus life, the real challenges of the future stared at him. For a pauper youth like him, education was primarily a means to earn livelihood. But in his State, Kerala, where the literacy rate is 95% and unemployment rate 15%, there was nothing bright for him to dream of. One gets placement not just because of his academic merit and skill, but based on the political and financial influence one can exert. Unfortunately, Krishnan had neither money nor political connections. His father had already retired and his meagre pension of Rs. 15000 was the sole income of the family for their sustenance. Krishnan was compelled to seek some job and help his father in maintaining the family.

He applied for whatever job opportunities he was eligible for—from last grade post to officer level. The government tests, interviews and appointment took much time, even years. He decided to tutor classes for pupils and students. He had some command of English, and that helped him to tutor both school pupils and college students. He could also teach classes on social studies, but no pupil needed it. English always is nightmare for ordinary Indian students, and hence there was much opportunity for him to teach them in mornings and evenings both before and after school hours. From early morning till 9 am and from 4.30 pm to 8 pm, Krishnan held classes in the students' houses. He taught history and economics in a parallel college from 10 am to 4 pm. He could earn Rs. 15,000 monthly altogether through these classes.

Years passed, one after another, and Krishnan's longing and prayer for a government job also passed unheeded by the Creator. Krishnan was now thirty, and his mother became almost bedridden due to arthritis. Fortunately, father was healthy enough to manage the domestic duties of cooking, cleaning and so on. The family was not in a position to keep a maidservant as she would have needed a minimum Rs. 10000 as her monthly salary. Krishnan's father and mother pressured him to marry, but Krishnan replied, "Dear dad, how can I afford to have another member in this family when my earnings are so low? Being a self-employed man, I can't expect a partner who is government employed. For ma's treatment, we have additional expenses."

"Ok, son, it will be as you decide," father said.

"But how long will you stay single, son? You are already thirty now," mother replied.

"Let's wait, ma. Maybe within a year I'll get a government job. I have sat so many Public Service Commission tests!"

The reply from his mother was only a deep sigh and whisper: "Lord Krishna save us!"

Time doesn't wait for Krishnan to get a government job. Krishnan entered into his thirty-third year. Mother's condition was worsening and father also showed the symptoms of old age. Finally Krishnan consented to marry. Being an ideal youth, he was against the dowry system and wanted to marry a poor girl who had graduated from college. He hated the caste system and wanted his bride to belong to a backward community. Fortunately his parents were never against his wishes and views. Thus he registered his name in KeralaMatrimonial.com, showing his familial, professional, and financial details, and his expectancies of the bride's qualities and educational qualifications.

Being a self-employed youth, he was less marketable in the matrimonial world, but since his expectations were affordable for poor girls, he got some proposals. He selected a girl named Seetha, who was fair enough, and had a post-graduate degree in English literature. No doubt she, too, was unemployed and taught in some tutoring centre. Krishnan's and Seetha's wedding took place in a very simple manner in the Registrar's Office near to his house and the guests and friends, very few in number, were given a simple dinner in a hotel.

Krishnan continued his teaching as a home tutor, as well as in the parallel college, and Seetha remained in the house as a housewife doing all domestic duties and serving as a nurse to her mother-in-law. Krishnan's hope of getting a government job was waning, but still he continued to apply for the Kerala Public Service Commission's tests. The tests were becoming tougher and tougher to eliminate as many candidates as possible from the hundreds of thousands who applied. A daughter was born to Krishnan and Seetha two years after their marriage. And a son also was born after another three years. Destiny continued to wound Krishnan, and Seetha showed symptoms of liver cirrhosis. The treatment was very costly and Krishnan took a loan from a bank, pledging their ancestral property.

At last God heeded Krishnan's and his family's prayer. He got an appointment as a lower division clerk in the revenue department at the age of 38. Maybe he was considered taking into consideration his upper age limit. After 36, one can't apply for PSC tests. The postman brought the appointment letter on a Saturday when Krishnan was there in his house. Saturdays were holidays for the college where he taught. He was exhilarated when he opened the envelope. He shared the happy news with his parents and wife. They were all jubilant.

Krishnan got down at the town at 9.30 am, and took an auto rickshaw to the Taluk Office. The office was open, but no one was there. He waited there on the veranda. By 10 am, the staff had strolled into the office, one after another. When they were settled on their seats, Krishnan approached the person seated near to the entrance door. There were heaps of files on the table before him.

"Sir, I have come to join as a Lower Division Clerk in this office," he said, showing the appointment order.

"Go and meet the Tahsildar in that cabin."

Krishnan went to the cabin and greeted the tax officer, a grey-haired man.

"Good morning Sir. My name is Krishnan Namboodiri and I have come to join this office." he handed the appointment order over.

Looking at the appointment order, the Tahsildar asked him to sit. He asked about Krishnan's home location. Then he took the attendance register and entered Krishnan's name and asked him to sign it.

"Krishnan, this office is going very smoothly with few complaints from the public. So, you have to do your duties very promptly as others do. There is harmony in our work and therein lies our success. Ask me or the section clerk near to your table if you have any questions regarding the filing system."

"Surely Sir, I will be very dutiful in my work," Krishnan replied.

The Tahsildar then called the peon and asked him to show Krishnan's seat. Krishnan was led to a chair and a table heaped with dusty files. Thus started Krishnan's office life. The section clerks seated nearby introduced themselves to him and extended all help.

Krishnan could learn his section work very easily. The junior super-intendent who was his section head was a man of few words although rather a nagging character. Loving words never came from his mouth.

After a month in the office, Krishnan became friendly with other clerks, and assessed their character. He was the only one in the office with a post-graduate degree. He found that the entire staff was lazy in their work, but greedy for bribes. He could find, on some days, the peon serving small envelopes to the section clerks and others. He guessed that the envelopes contained currency, since he heard the section clerk nearby to him asking the peon how much was there in it.

A week later, the peon was serving the envelopes and he offered one to Krishnan. "What's it Raju?" Krishnan asked the peon.

"It's a tip from some generous customer, Sir."

"Sorry, I can't take it. I don't want any presents for my duty."

"Sir, this is the practice in our office. Everyone is getting a share."

"I call it bribe and I am against such a practice."

"In that case, I will have to report to the Tahsildar. Sir, unless you accept it, you may be transferred. It happened to some lady clerk a few years back."

"Sorry, I can't do anything against my conscience."

The peon reported the matter to the Tahsildar and immediately Krishnan was called to him.

"Krishnan, don't pretend to be like Lord Krishna. I told you on the very first day that you will have to cooperate with us and go in harmony. These petty amounts are presents given to us very happily by the customers for the service we render to them. We haven't asked them any fee or reward," the Tahsildar said.

"Sorry Sir, I call it bribe. Even if they give them unasked, we are not bound to accept it. We are paid by the government for our work. I believe it is the people's money through taxes which we are getting as salary and we are bound to serve them for free in return."

"I don't want to argue with you. There is a staff of twenty-two in this office and none of them finds any wrong in accepting these compliments. You will have to bear the consequences if you swim against the flow of this office."

"Sorry Sir, I can't tolerate it. My conscience doesn't allow me."

"OK, you may go to your seat."

Krishnan went to his seat, quite upset. Then other section clerks one by one came to him and asked to change his decision. The superintendents called him to their seats and advised him. But Krishnan couldn't change his decision and accept the envelope.

Reaching home, Krishnan told his parents and wife what had happened in the office.

Seetha said, "What will we do IF they transfer you to some distant place? Ma and I are sick. Father can't manage the household activities alone."

Then father said, "Seetha, do you want him to be corrupt? Whatever be the consequences, dear son, don't accept such money." Mother also supported father's words.

"Dad, I never want my husband to be corrupt. I just reminded him of the possible consequences," Seetha replied.

"Daughter, we will manage somehow. God is with us," father said.

As expected and feared, Krishnan got the transfer order after a week. He was transferred to a village office at a remote place in the high ranges. Krishnan was unmoved. He decided to file a complaint in the high court after joining the village office. He was given full support from his parents and wife. He had to stay in a house near the village office as a paying guest. Fighting against the chilly weather, Krishnan continued his work in the office, serving poor people of the locality. They were given the certificates and other needed documents as quickly as possible. He could work in the office in the late evenings and expedite the service. Fortunately, the village tax officer was also an honest, service-minded man.

Krishnan filed a bribery case in the high court against the Tahsildar and the entire staff of the Taluk Office. As a student, he had pledged that he would fight against bribery when a chance came. He pawned Seetha's gold to meet the advocate's fees. He had already recorded in his cell phone the talks between him and the peon, the Tahsilar, the superintendents and other clerks and other staffs in the Taluk Office regarding the cash envelope which he'd rejected. He produced the voice recordings as evidence to the advocate.

The trial date came after a month, and he was interrogated by his own advocate and the respondents' advocate and finally the judge himself. Also, the entire staff of the Taluk Office and even a few customers who gave them bribes were interrogated by Krishnan's advocate. There was clear evidence of the bribery. which the entire staff had been accepting from the customers. The judge pronounced the verdict. He requested the government to transfer the entire staff of the Taulk Office to remote areas and cut their future increments for two years. In addition, each one of them was required to pay a fine ranging from Rs. 50,000 to 10,000, based on their designation, from which Krishnan would be given Rs. 200,000 as a reward for his fearless fight against corruption. Moreover, Krishnan should be transferred to his hometown with an additional increment to his salary.

The news of the verdict covered the front page of all newspapers and flashed as hot news of all TV channels. Thus Krishnan became a hero. He was given a warm reception by the Governor of Kerala where he was awarded the BEST GOVERNMENT SERVANT.

~ ~ ~

5 – Joseph's Maiden Vote for Parliament

"Pappa, I am going to cast my maiden vote for parliament tomorrow. But whom to vote is the problem now," Joseph told his father, Thomas.

"Good, my son. Thus you are going to become part of the administration of the country. Since ours is a democratic country, we citizens are to be very vigilant in electing our representatives. You are politically educated and so I need not suggest any candidate's name," Thomas replied.

Thomas was a leading Advocate in the High Court. His son, Joseph, was a Bachelor of Technology student in the government engineering College at Kochi. Thomas' wife, Mercy, was a professor in a government college at Kochi itself. They had a daughter, Jane, who was in high school.

"Pappa, do you think democracy is the best form of government? How far is our democracy from the original concept? Where do you find equality, fraternity and liberty in our country? Isn't communism better than this?" Joseph continued.

"My son, communism is a great philosophy, as democracy is. But it is impractical and utopian in this materialistic world. Man is innately selfish and hence no one works for the common welfare. That's the reason why it failed in Russia and the eastern European countries. Do you think China is a pure communist country? No. In fact, it is capitalistic, just like western capitalistic countries. Joseph, it's time for me to go the court. We shall discuss the matter in detail when I come back." Thomas got into his Maruthi car and drove away.

Joseph was enjoying his vacation after his third semester examinations. Jane was getting ready to go to school.

Mercy, dressed in a blue sari, came near her son and said, "Son, I am going to the college. See that the front door is locked always because thieves may come at any time."

"Ma, please wait. I am also coming," Jane cried.

"Hurry up. It's already late," Mercy replied.

Joseph, all alone in the house, started thinking about elections, democracy, corruption etc. Sixty-four long years have passed since the country got its independence. What is there to be proud of? Number two in world population? Where is the growth those politicians and administrators boasted of? *India is becoming a superpower in growth! We will outrun America and Japan!* Aren't the political mafia eye-washing the innocent, illiterate masses? A UN study reported India's per capita income as Rs. 20. Isn't the gap between the rich and the poor becoming wider and wider? Could these politicians reduce the illiteracy of the masses? Aren't they actually fostering ignorance and illiteracy of the villagers to exploit them to the hilt? Do they ever think of the dreams of the youth here? Where are the employment opportunities when young people graduate from their educational institutions? Joseph became restless as he voyaged through these dark realities. He shut his eyes and remained on his chair on the front veranda, trying to cool himself down. Suddenly a group of men in white attire flocked to the house with election notices in their hands.

"We have come with the voter's slips. Where are the father and mother of this household?" one man with the voters list asked.

"They're at work," Joseph replied.

They gave him three slips—father's mother's and Joseph's. "Joseph, don't forget to vote for our candidate," another man said.

"Why should I vote for your candidate? What's your Front doing at the Centre? 2G Spectrum corruption, Adarsh Housing corruption, Commonwealth Games corruption! How many crores? Three lakh crore rupees! Whose money is it? Poor farmers and labourers! Isn't your government trying to protect the criminal ministers? If the money thus lost were retrieved from them, the country could feed the poor people for next five years! Why doesn't the government reveal the names of the account holders in foreign banks who have amassed five hundred billion dollars through unfair means? Even after forty years, why is it that the Lokpal Bill is not passed by the parliament? Thanks to Anna Hazare, the movement has started now. A second independence struggle is the need of the day. I won't vote for your candidate and thus promote corruption," Joseph exploded. His mind was just a sea mounting with violent waves flinging pebbles at the shore. The campaigners were literally stunned.

They had nothing to say. "OK, boy you may vote for anyone you like," one of them whispered and they fled from the house.

Joseph felt much relieved and relaxed. He laughed loudly and told himself, "Well done Joseph! You couldn't say those things to the prime minister or the president." He got into the drawing room, shutting the front door behind him. He planned to go to the library to return the books and take out a few more. As he was dressing, he heard the sound of the doorbell. Immediately, he put a shirt on and opened the front door. Oh! Another group of election campaigners!

"We have got the slips," Joseph told them with an impatient tone.

"Take our slips also and vote to our candidate," one of them said.

"You are the people who are playing the communal card. India is a secular state and all religions have equal rights here. No preference for majority or minority. There is no such thing as an ethnic or national heritage. In this multicultural society, religious sentiments should give way to national sentiments or even global sentiments," Joseph was positively bellowing rhetoric and he saw the group retreating. Someone was saying, "This boy is mad! Let's not waste our time here."

Joseph again laughed and congratulated himself. He took the library books and went in the direction of the library. On the way he found the parish priest in front of the church.

"Joseph, where are you going?"

"To the library, Father. Father, I don't understand why the Church is interfering in politics. Why is such a pastoral letter read in all the churches? Let the laymen vote for anyone they like. It is dangerous to mix politics with religion," Joseph said.

"Joseph, we have to elect men who protect our faith. Communists are atheists and they mustn't be elected. That's why such a letter was read in the churches," the priest replied.

"Father, ours is a secular state and no MP can act against secularism. There is the Supreme Court to look into such matters. If members are elected on the basis of religion rather than their merits, the parliament will be a pandemonium of religious fanatics. Parliament is a place to discuss national issues," Joseph retorted.

"I am no one to argue with you, Joseph. I was asked to read the pastoral letter and I did. That's all," the priest had nothing else to tell him.

Bidding goodbye to the priest, Joseph continued his walk. He took out some new books from the library and returned home. After lunch, he dove into the books and time passed unaware. His ma returned from the college and he told the day's proceedings. Mercy reprimanded him for talking roughly to the campaigners and the priest.

"My son, you don't know how these irrational people will react. They are all crazy from this election and are ready to go to any extreme for their party and the candidate," Mercy reminded him.

Thomas arrived home at seven in the evening. Joseph told his father how he had reacted to the campaigners and priest. Thomas too cautioned him for his overreacting.

"Joseph, corruption is part of modern democracy. Only through a mass movement can this social evil be wiped out. It is futile to fight against it singlehandedly. We do need a government here. What alternative is there for democracy? Monarchy? Don't you see the civil war that took place in Egypt and now going on in Libya, Syria and Yemen where monarchy prevails?" Thomas explained.

"But Pappa, a presidential form of democracy as we find in America is far better than ours. There is less corruption there, I believe," Joseph replied.

"True. But our politicians may not opt for it because they couldn't keep exploiting the people as they are doing now," Thomas responded.

"Pappa, who shall I vote for? I don't find anyone worthy," Joseph said.

"Son, at the polling station, your mind will you. Act accordingly," Thomas concluded.

Supper being over, they went to sleep. Joseph's mind was disturbed still. The thought of his maiden vote was biting him like a mosquito. Tired of drinking sufficient blood from him the mosquito flew away and Sleep conquered him at midnight.

Mercy awoke him. "Joseph, get up. It's already seven in the morning. You have to cast your maiden vote. Get ready soon before there is heavy rush at the booth."

Thomas, Mercy and Joseph walked to the polling station, because it was only half a kilometre away. There wasn't a long queue, only some fifteen voters. After father's and mother's vote, Joseph got into the station. He gave the slip to the first polling officer. His name was read aloud to the polling agents and other polling officers. His signature was obtained on the register and indelible ink was marked on the left forefinger. The third polling officer pressed the switch of the ballot machine's control unit and asked Joseph to move to the balloting unit placed in the voting compartment. Joseph went through the names of the candidates and their symbols on the voting machine. *Who to vote for?* He asked his mind. His mind was not responding. Reports of the multibillion corruptions by the central ministers went through his mind like on a movie. He became very pset.

"What are you doing there? Press the button and leave," the presiding officer told him loudly. Joseph still remained like a statue. "Hey, can't you hear what I say? Vote and go out," the presiding officer shouted.

"I don't want to cast my vote for any of these candidates. Where is the button for it?" Joseph exploded.

"There is no button for it," getting from his seat the presiding officer replied angrily.

"I don't want to vote for traitors," Joseph roared. "Political mafia Murdabad! Anna Hazare Zindabad! (Down with political mafia! Long live Anna Hazare) Political mafia Murdabad! Anna Hazare Zindabad!" raising his right fist up Joseph thundered and ran out of the station. His slogan echoed from the neighbouring hills.

~ ~ ~

6 – School Entrance Festival

Dear readers, I am going to present before you a story that is the reality of my own State, Kerala, the most literate one, situated in the southern part of India.

Vidya is five years old now. She has a younger brother aged three. Her father and mother are construction labourers. But the father deserted the family two years ago, and lives with another woman. The mother continued looking after the children while to working. They lived in a rented hut, paying Rs. 1000 per month.

Life became even harder for them, because the mother developed diabetes, and is no longer able to work. The family is cared for by her poor old parents and her brother who is an auto rickshaw driver.

When Vidya was forced to attend an *anganwadi* (child service centre of the central government), her friends in the neighbourhood studied in LKGs and UKGs[1] run by upper-class private companies. She had to walk two kilometres to reach her anganwadi, which was just a makeshift cowshed. Her mates there were all like her, coming from very poor families, clad in cheap clothes. Vidya could only dream of the gaudy, high quality clothes her friends in the neighbourhood wore to school. She looked with thirsty eyes the way her neighbour tots went in dazzling school uniforms and tempting bags to their schools in the town in their school buses. They all had five or more pairs of uniforms, whereas she had to be content with only two, which were faded and torn. Vidya could get lunch from the anganwadi—rice and lentil curry—the chief temptation for all the little ones there. She would bring some rice and curry for her brother too, which her teacher was kind enough to supply, after learning of the pathetic condition of her home.

Now I shall draw your attention to St. Mark's High School, a government assisted[2] corporate managed school in the town. It had a proud

____

[1] LKG stands for Lower Kindergarten. Kindergarten specifies a babysitter or nursery school for the children of 3-4 years old. In the Indian education system, there are 3 years of elementary education before primary school. These three years are Nursery, LKG (Lower Kindergarten), and UKG (Upper Kindergarten).

[2] See note at end of chapter for an explanation of *aided schools*.

profile in the glorious past—a model school for other schools in the State. There were 1500 pupils with five divisions, each from first standard to tenth, and there were more than 60 teachers. One hundred percent passed in the Secondary School Leaving Certificate (SSLC) examinations. Ironically, the present state of the school was very deplorable. The school had become 'uneconomic' and under the constant threat of closure. Attendance had fallen to fifty pupils and fifteen teachers and single division to all standards. The school could still maintain the hundred percent result for the SSLC, but there were only five candidates.

The manager of the school, Fr. Philipose, called an urgent staff meeting. The headmaster and teachers assembled in the staffroom. The meeting started after a silent prayer.

"Respected Headmaster and my dear teachers," the manager opened the discussion. "The school will reopen next week after the vacation. First of June is the entrance fest. We haven't got any pupils for the first standard. Last year we could get a child somehow. What will we do? We will lose the first standard and that will be the first death knell to the school."

One of the teachers, Chako said, "Let Smitha, the teacher who is in charge of the first standard, find tots from somewhere. Our teachers and the management are responsible for the present pathetic situation. The teachers should have sent their children to this school and thus showed a model to all parents. Where have their children studied except mine? They were sent to Central Board of Secondary Education (CBSE) English medium private schools. To make things worse, our corporate management also started such unaided schools. Pupils' numbers are decreasing every year as part of population control, but the numbers of unaided schools are increasing. Education has become the most profitable business,"

"What Chacko sir said is true. It is hypocritical for you to meet the poor parents and ask for their children," the manger continued. "Even when the corporate management has opened unaided schools, you should have sent your children to your own school. Now you may collectively search for a pupil or two just to retain our first standard. Teacher Smitha can't get one all by herself. Tomorrow, you all have to go, under the leadership of the headmaster, to the houses of the poor where little children haven't yet enrolled in a school."

"We shall do as Father has requested," the headmaster said. "Getting a pupil is just like buying one. We will have to spend for it as we did last year. Whatever the demand from the parents, we have to accept it. Let's accept collective responsibility and we will divide the expense among us."

All the teachers agreed to this suggestion, and the next day, the whole staff set out in the neighbourhood in search of tots for the first standard. Being local teachers, they knew very well which houses had young children. They visited these houses one after another, but the little children in those houses had already joined CBSE English medium schools, paying a large amount as admission fee, tuition fee, PTA fund, anniversary fee etc. Finally they came to Vidya's house. Vidya's mother and brother could understand sufficiently early the high demand for their child, since she was the only one in the neighbourhood who was forced to study in any Malayalam medium aided/government school. They had also learned how the present pupil in the second standard was given all facilities including financial help to the family last year.

"Sister, we are teachers of St. Mark's High School," the headmaster said. "We have learnt that your child is of age to attend the first standard. We request you to send her to our school."

"True, our Vidya is five years old and has to enrol in some school. Have you got any other child for the first standard?" the mother asked.

"None, but we are seeking," the headmaster said.

"If we could afford to, we would have sent her to an English medium school in the town. We are poor people, unlike you. You who are seeking pupils now for your school never sent your own children to your school. Why, because you have no faith in your teaching and the standard of your school. You didn't want to risk your children's education and future. You are now running for your own protection of service and high salary. Sorry, you are all educated people and who am I to speak to you so. Teachers from other aided Lower Primary schools[3] as well as those of government High school in the town approached us yesterday and the day before yesterday. They offered the child three sets of uniforms, a school bag, an umbrella and free conveyance. Do you know how we live here? I am a diabetic patient and can't do any work. We survive thanks to my brother,

---

[3] In the Indian school education system, there are four levels. From First Standard (1st grade in the USA) to Fourth Standard is called Lower Primary. From Fifth Standard to Seventh Standard is called Upper Primary. From Eighth Standard to Tenth Standard is called High School (HS) or Secondary. 11th and 12th Standard consists of Higher Secondary (HSS) or Plus Two (10+2).

Depending on locale, there may be separate schools for each level as well as all the three or four levels together in a campus under one administration.

who is an auto rickshaw driver. I need injections every day. If you can meet our family's expenses as well as what the child needs, we shall give you our child."

"How much do you need a month, for food and medicine? Kindly don't exploit us but calculate just for your necessities," the headmaster said.

"We are using ration rice from the government shop and never go for any delicacies. For food we need Rs. 5000, rent Rs. 1000 and Rs. 2000 for my medicine. Vidya can't walk alone all the two kilometres to the school. So an auto rickshaw has to be arranged for her which needs Rs. 2000. So if you give us Rs. 10000 per month we will give you our child. In addition, you have to give her three sets of uniforms, school bag and an umbrella. I am requesting only the bare minimum since you are all my native teachers."

"OK, we agree. Take this as June's charge in advance." The headmaster gave the mother Rs. 10000 from his wallet. "Where is Vidya? Kindly call her."

"She is playing with her friends in the neighbourhood. I will call her right now," the mother said.

"Vidya, please come here. Your teachers have come," she called out.

Vidya came running, with a sweating face. She blushed when she saw such a group of teachers.

"Vidya, these are your teachers. You are going to enrol in the first standard of St. Mark's High School," mother told her.

"Who will my friends be there?" Vidya asked.

There was silence for some time. The headmaster then told her, "Sure, you will have friends there." Poor Vidya believed those words. "Vidya take this," Smitha teacher took a packet of sweets from her bag and gave to her. Vidya's face beamed with joy when she received the packet.

"Next Monday is the reopening day of the school and there is entrance festival. You should come with Vidya by 9.45 am. She will be given new uniform, a bag, textbooks and notebooks and an umbrella by the school manager. If Vidya doesn't have a new dress now, we will bring a pair within two days," the headmaster continued.

"She has no good dress, sir," mother replied.

"Then we will bring it day after tomorrow."

By 9.45 am on Monday, Vidya and her mother arrived at the school in her new dress, in her uncle's auto rickshaw. As part of the entrance festival, the front gate of the school was decorated with a palm leaf arch and multicoloured balloons. When the first bell rang, all the fifty pupils of the school in their uniforms assembled in two rows at the entrance of the school to receive the new member, Vidya. Little ones of the LP level were holding balloons in their hands, while pupils of the UP and HS were carrying bouquets of flowers. The headmaster, teachers and school leader marched to the gate to receive Vidya. The school leader, Jasmine, was in the front. She gave a big beautiful bouquet of flowers to Vidya and they marched back to the headmaster's room while pupils on either side of them showered petals of flowers on Vidya. Just like a guard of honour to a VIP, Vidya was led to the headmaster's room. The manger, Fr. Philipose, was there in the headmaster's room and he received Vidya with presents of chocolates, uniforms, a bag and an umbrella. Vidya was highly elated. She was then taken by Smitha teacher to her class. The class was decorated with flowers and balloons. There were a few small chairs for the children.

"Teacher, where are the other pupils? Am I alone?" Vidya asked, a bit dejected,.

Smitha teacher told a lie: "No Vidya. Others will join tomorrow."

Yes, Vidya's school life started. For the next ten months she was be alone in her class with her teacher, Smitha. For Smitha teacher it was a great relief for she could continue there without being transferred to some other remote school of the corporate management. Her salary of Rs. 40000 per month was protected by the government for teaching just one pupil. It's not a lone case in Kerala. There are hundreds of Vidyas and Smitha teachers in thousands of schools across the State.

~ ~ ~

According to the RTI information gathered by an NGO All-India Save Education Committee, there are currently 2,577 schools in the State that have less than 50 students on their rolls. Out of these, 1,217 are government schools and 1,360 are aided schools. Interestingly, there are seven Lower Primary Schools in the State, which do not have even a single student. While four schools have one student each on their rolls, the number of schools having less than 10 students is 109. According to a circular of the Department of General Education in 2012, schools from lower primary to high school-level, which have less than 60 students (average of 15 students in a class) are termed uneconomic. (*The New Indian Express* 31 May 2014).

Aided Schools – An Explanation

In government schools, the teachers are appointed by the government, conducting tests and interviews and they are given a monthly salary by the government. The building and infrastructure is the government's. In aided schools (Govt. aided schools), the selection of the teachers is done by the private management who owns the building and campus and infrastructure. The salary of the teachers, equivalent of the government school teachers, is given by the government. Also, grants are made to the management for the maintenance of the school building. Hence these kinds of schools are called *aided schools*.

Since the government is not able to buy and own these schools, the appointing authority is given to the private management, and they make a huge profit through the appointment of teachers and other staff through bribes. In fact, these schools were built by public money collected by individual management, or by corporate management. Thus, education has become one of the most profitable business in Kerala and other States. In government schools and aided schools, the pupils need not pay any fee. In contrast, in private English medium instruction schools, pupils have to pay huge fees, and the teachers appointed there by the management are paid a low salary collected from the fees of the pupils. The government has less control over them.

~ ~ ~

7 – Mother Tongue Impact

This story takes place in my own state, Kerala, the southern State of Multilingual India. Popularly known among tourists as 'God's own country,' Kerala has special characteristics of its own—equable climate, full of greenery, 100 percent education, etc. Along with the positive qualities of literacy, cleanliness, secularism, the people are notorious for laziness, vanity, and egocentrism.

Unlike the people of the other States, Keralites have an unrivalled mind in projecting their false pride in the construction of their houses, use of vehicles, education of their children, and so on. Even a person whose income is small, and who is doomed to debt till death, will try to construct a palatial house, double storied or even more in order to outshine the neighbour. Similarly, one's car(s)—in luxurious quality as well as in number, have the purpose of outshining the neighbour.

The most deplorable is the vanity shown in the education of the family's children. Not thinking about the negative impact or the indirect cruelty shown to their offspring, they compel them to study in an English medium[4] private school just because their neighbours' children study in such big shots' costly schools.

Here is a story related to that kind of education in Kerala. More than 50% of the enrolled pupils in Kerala are in English medium schools, when there are innumerable government and government aided Malayalam (mother tongue) medium schools in all the villages. In several other States, the parents are compelled to send their pupils to English medium schools when mother tongue medium government schools are absent in their areas.

Dr. Manoj, Madhu and Mahesh are neighbours and live with their families in the housing colony at Kottayam. While Dr. Manoj lives with his wife, Dr. Sheela, and two children in a high cost double storeyed house, Madhu, a lover division clerk in the education department lives with his unemployed wife, Aswathy, and their only son in a middle priced single storied house. Mahesh is an auto rickshaw driver, and lives with his

---

[4] Medium in the sense that English language is the *medium* of instruction.

jobless wife, Seetha, and two children in a low cost single bedroom house. A housewife's never-ending work in a house is never considered an employment by the government and society, since it doesn't earn money. Dr. Manoj's son Rajiv studies in the eighth standard of the English medium private school in the town, where children of the elite are sent.

For Dr. Manoj, the son's education is never a financial burden, since he and his wife are doctors in the government hospital, besides having a private practice in their house. They want their son to become a doctor and follow their profession. Madhu and his wife Aswathy are representatives of the characteristically vainglorious Keralites, and they sent their son Sankar to the same English medium school, paying high fees. Sankar studies in the same class as Rajiv.

Mahesh and Seetha, too, longed for their son Vishnu's education in the same English medium school, but since their income is so low, they've had to sacrifice their longing and sent Vishnu to a government school in the town where no fees had to be paid. Unlike many other government schools of the State, Govt. High School, Kottayam is a model school where the teachers are committed and the infrastructure is good. Vishnu is of the same age of Rajiv and Sankar, and studies at the eighth standard.

The present education system has come to such an unpleasant state that pupils have little time for recreation, physical exercise, and the simple pleasures of playing sports. They don't even have time to chat. Early in the morning, they have to get up, finish the homework and study the lessons taught the previous day, attend home tutors for difficult subjects, go to school, return home after class, again tutoring classes, study, homework, till 10 or 11pm when they go to bed. After return from school, Rajiv, Sankar and Vishnu used to chat for some fifteen minutes, which their parents permitted them.

When Rajiv and Sankar heard of the jolly atmosphere of Vishnu's school—how the pupils in that school enjoy their study and take part in sports and games and extra-curricular activities; how easily they can study the lessons since the medium of instruction is Malayalam; and they are free to communicate in their mother tongue; not overburdened by much homework or tuition; how Vishnu gets time to watch TV and sleep as much as he likes—they couldn't but envy him.

One evening returning after the usual chat with Vishnu, Rajiv told his father, "Papa, why didn't you send me to the government school where Vishnu studies? How happy he is! He doesn't need to worry about study.

He is enjoying his school life, while I am overburdened by homework, tuitions, studies, without any rest at all."

Dr. Manoj replied, "What nonsense are you speaking, Rajiv? Bear in mind that you are the son of doctors. And what should you become in future? Not less than a doctor. Unless you study in such a high-standard English medium school, you can't attain the goal. And what is Vishnu compared to you? His father is only an illiterate auto rickshaw driver. Vishnu can't dream of a doctor's profession, so he is studying in the poor people's government school. Unless you study hard, you can't become a doctor."

Rajiv didn't respond to what his father said and went quietly to his room. He knew very well that his parents would never allow him to study in a government school and mingle with ordinary children.

Sankar also complained to his mother one day. "Mummy, I am tired of studying in the English medium school. I can't understand what the teachers are teaching. They don't explain the subjects in Malayalam and I have to learn by heart the texts and the notes the teachers assign. I don't get enough sleep after the homework and study. Today, the headmaster caned me for speaking a Malayalam sentence to one of my classmates. The leader overheard it and told it to the class teacher, who in turn reported it to the headmaster. There aren't any days I am not punished by the teachers for not giving the correct answers to their questions. Unless I understand what they teach, how can I study and answer? Mummy, compare my school life with Vishnu's. How happy he is, do you know? He is never punished. He is top in the class. He doesn't have to pay any fees in the school, while how much we are giving as fees? Mummy, I will become number one in the class if I am admitted in Vishnu's school. I am now ranked 40th among the fifty pupils in our class."

Sankar's mother Aswathy exploded, "Don't speak such nonsense, my dear son. We want to make you a doctor. You should always long for a higher level. What are Vishnu and his parents? Do you want to become an auto rickshaw driver like Vishnu's father? Why don't you learn from your classmate, Rajiv? He is one of the top pupils in the class. Whatever atmosphere and facilities are there for his study in his house, we have arranged such for you also in our house. Then why can't you study like him?"

Sankar replied, "Mummy, I am not Rajiv. His parents are doctors, and what about mine? Naturally, his IQ will be higher than mine. If he has any doubt in any subject, his parents are literate enough to explain it."

Aswathy said, "Are you ashamed of your parents, then? Don't you know how much we are financially struggling to give you a good education? True, we are not able to clear help with your schoolwork, but we have arranged tuition masters for you. You should ask them to instruct you,"

"I am doing my best, dear mummy. I'm just unable to memorise all notes and answers. The notes I learn by heart today I will forget a week after. What shall I do then? In Malayalam medium schools, there is nothing to be learnt by heart. Once we understand the things well, it will remain in the mind and we can reproduce it whenever needed. What Vishnu studies in Malayalam is the same thing we study in English. I mean the subjects of mathematics, science and social studies. What difference is there in the knowledge we get and the pupils of Malayalam medium schools get? In fact, they acquire more knowledge than we pupils who learn everything by heart like a parrot."

Aswathy retorted, "Whatever arguments you state, we won't send you to a government Malayalam medium school where poor pupils study. We have to keep up our prestige. You should live among high class pupils and communicate with them. It's better that you cut your friendship with Vishnu. He is a bad influence upon you and dissuades you from your studies. I am going to tell him and his parents not to have any connection with you."

"Mummy, Vishnu and his parents are very good people. Please don't say such hurtful words to them. If you insist, I will not interact with Vishnu any more. Please don't complain to them."

"OK, then, don't talk to him anymore or visit his house. I won't complain to them."

Sankar stopped visiting Vishnu and his house. Not finding Sankar the next day, Vishnu phoned him through his cell phone. When Sankar told the truth, Vishnu was shocked and wounded and they decided to continue their friendship through secretly via phone.

The overburden of studies and discipline at school started to affect the tender mind of Sankar, and he was often found reticent and moody. He did poorly in the terminal examinations, and the class teacher requested his parents to meet her. She showed the progress report to Aswathy. Sankar had failed in all the subject papers and passed only the language papers of Malayalam, English and Hindi. The class teacher warned Aswathy that if Sankar didn't improve in the next examinations, he would be expelled from the school. Reaching home, Aswathy scolded and even thrashed Sankar for his poor performance, and thereby bringing disgrace on her and the family.

When Madhu returned from the office, Aswathy reported the son's case to him. He also scolded the child, but did not beat him. Sankar was weeping all the night. He was unwilling to eat his supper, but Aswathy forced him to eat something, then he went to his bedroom. About midnight, he shrieked loudly. The parents ran to his room and asked him what had happened. Sankar was crying loudly, saying that in his dream the headmaster and other teachers were chasing him with canes in their hands. Madhu and Aswathy were deeply touched, and tried to console him. They took him to their bedroom and asked him to sleep with them. The lights were put out.

Sankar couldn't sleep and started yelling, "Papa, save me! They are coming again to beat me."

Madhu switched on the light and said, "My dear son, it is only a hallucination. How can your teachers come here during the night?" They are all sleeping in their houses."

"Papa, I can't go to that school. They will thrash me to death," Sankar cried.

"Ok, you need not go. Now try to sleep," Madhu tried to pacify him. All the night Sankar had a fever and delirious moans.

Early morning, Madhu and Aswathy took Sankar to the medical college and consulted the psychiatrist. The doctor made a thorough case study, interrogating the parents and Sankar separately. Then in the presence of Sankar the doctor asked the parents, "Do you want your child to regain his normalcy?"

"Surely, sir. We have no other child and we live for him," Madhu replied.

"Then why don't you grant his wish?" the doctor continued. "He has told you several times that he is not able to follow the classes in that English medium school. And the examinations proved that he is totally unfit to be there. You say that you want to make him a doctor. The nation and society need not only doctors but countless types of officers and employees in different sectors of services. And if you are so particular of the profession of doctors, he can get selection in the entrance test for MBBS even if he studies in the Malayalam medium school. Hundreds of Malayalam medium students get selected in the entrance test every year. Sankar has promised that he will rank top if he is admitted in the Malayalam medium school. Why don't you try it, then? The only way to cure him now is to admit him in the government Malayalam medium school immediately. In addition, I shall prescribe some tonic and a few tablets, which will help him soon."

Both the parents agreed to the doctor's advice and decided to send Sankar in the government school. Hearing this, Sankar became very happy and expressed his gratitude to the doctor and his parents, "Thank you doctor, thank you papa, thank you mummy. I promise you, that I'll become number one in the new school and as you wish I will try my best to become a doctor."

Hearing this, the parents became very happy and kissed him on his forehead. The next day, they went with him to his school, and requested the headmaster for his transfer certificate. The headmaster and the teachers were greatly relieved to hear that Sankar was leaving the school and thus saving them from the disgrace of losing their high ranking in the 10th class examinations.

The headmaster of the Government High School was immensely happy when Sankar was brought before him to be admitted in the 8th standard. There was a shortage of pupils in all the classes. Thus Sankar joined with his friend Vishnu and both were ecstatic to sit beside each other.

Keeping his promise, Sankar ranked first in the next examination, as well as in the annual exams. He continued his best performance in the following years and was the top in the ninth standard as well as in the tenth standard. In the career-deciding 10th class final examinations, he topped the district and was honoured by the minister for education. Sankar studied the Plus Two course in the government higher secondary school at Kottayam. He won third rank in the State in the Plus Two examinations. In the entrance test to the MBBS course, he was ranked 15th and got admission in the medical college at Kottayam itself in the government quota with very minimum fees to be paid.

His classmate Vishnu also got a high ranking in the entrance test and admission in the government medical college at Thiruvananthapuram. Rajiv, who studied in the English medium private school couldn't get a high enough rank in the entrance examination and had to seek admission for MBBS in the management quota in a private management medical college, paying several lakhs of rupees as donation and fees.

Thus mother tongue medium educated Sankar and Vishnu have proved and proclaimed to the world that education in mother tongue brings out the best performance in studies, as well as acquisition of maximum knowledge.

8 – I am Unwanted

Here is a short story, which has a fusion of history and fiction. It took place in the State of Madhya Pradesh in India.

Let me start my autobiographical account from my high school days in the government school in our village. You will be laughing or shocked when you hear my name. My parents gave me the name 'Avaanchhit,' which in our mother tongue Hindi means 'Unwanted.' In my childhood, when parents and others called me this name, I didn't know its meaning. But when I entered high school, my classmates started to ridicule me, saying that "you are an unwanted daughter of your parents." Even the teachers were startled at the name, and asked me who was responsible for it. Then with a bleeding heart I asked my mother, "Ma, why did you give me such a funny, taunting, ridiculous name? I am laughed at by the pupils in our school, and even by my own teachers."

"We are really sorry, dear child. Your father and I were advised by our relatives that if you were given the name 'Avaanchhit,' I would give birth to a son after you," mother replied.

"That means I and all my five elder sisters were your unwanted children. And you couldn't have your desired son after me. So, my younger sister is also unwanted by you. Ma, you being a woman like me, how could you think of us as unwanted?"

I wanted to curse my parents. On a rethinking, I understood the mental disposition of my illiterate parents. I learnt the truth that not only my parents but almost all parents in our country long for male children rather than female. The reason is that a son is a boon to the parents in the material sense that he may bring wealth to the family by way of a dowry when he is married. Naturally, a daughter is a burden to the parents, because they will have to find a huge amount to give as dowry when she is given in marriage.

The fact that I am born as an unwanted being to my parents and to the world grieved me a lot, but my faith in the Creator gave me courage to take it as a challenge. I am sure that the Creator wanted me, and that's why He created me and sent me to this world. Unlike the earthly fathers and mothers, the divine Father does not discriminate against any of his children (creations). This reality disclosed God's intention in my creation and prompted me to do karma according to His will. I vowed to reveal to the world how wanted women are on earth.

I dropped my plan to change my name through gazette notification, and I decided to retain it despite the stigma. Since this gender discrimination is an offshoot of patriarchy, I decided to fight against it at an administrative level. With that ambition in mind, I studied hard, and came top in the examinations in school, undergraduate and postgraduate courses. I came out victorious in the Civil Services Examinations.

As I dreamed, I was posted as the District Collector of Anuppur District in Madhya Pradesh. Within the capacity of a Collector, with the resources collected from the State and the Central governments, I launched several schemes for the empowerment of women. Talks by eminent personalities and one day seminars were conducted in all the villages, and made the people aware of the role of women in society; the need for gender equality in education, employment, administration and politics; how sinful is foeticide and sexism; the need for the abolition of dowry system, and similar issues. The parents who give birth to daughters were honoured with an allowance Rs. 10000. The education expense of the female children was borne by the government. The dowry system was abolished from the district.

Avaanchhit's efforts for the empowerment of women brought tremendous results. A society that had hated newly born girl babies started loving them and even longed for their births. Avaanchhit was honoured by the State and Central governments as the best government servant. The schemes she implemented in her district were taken as models for the entire country and they were launched in all districts and States. Thus Avaanchhit proved through her life how wanted women are in a society.

~ ~ ~

9 – Our Dear Bhai

"Sandeep, Sir!"

I turned back and looked in the direction of the sound. I saw nobody except that young mango tree. Was it the sound of Bhai? I thought for a moment. I resumed listening to my colleague's chattering. "Sandeep, Sir," again the sound was heard from behind me. I turned and looked. But nobody was there.

"What are you looking at?" my colleague asked.

"Sir, didn't you hear Bhai calling me?"

"Bhai calling you? No, I didn't hear. Something wrong with your ears." He giggled.

"No, Sir. I heard him calling me twice."

"Might be a hallucination, Sandeep. Let me leave you a little early as I have some shopping to do. You may rest here until the body cools."

"OK, Sir. You may go. I will sit here for fifteen minutes until the sweating is over."

We'd been playing badminton, as has been our custom, for the past fifteen years. Once my colleague left, my mind took me to Bhai again. I searched for him in vain.

Rambahadur—we call him *Bhai*—is the watchman of our college. He is a Gurkha, aged 54. Characteristic of his race, Bhai is honest, brave, and 100 percent loyal. He is indeed our *bhai* (brother), an elder brother looking after us, our college and the premises from anti-social people. He is very loving and service-minded to the whole college community. He has no reluctance to do any duty—even a coolie's or menial's. While we teachers and non-teachers work only three to eight hours in the daytime, Bhai's duty is 24 hours, sleeping just four hours at night.

He has conquered not only the college community with his pure love, but also the whole town. Bhai is known to all people in the town, young and old. Though he is illiterate, he can be sent on errant to any nook and cranny of the country. During feasts and celebrations in the college, he is at the forefront, serving food and compelling us to eat more and more. He always has the adage that our happiness is his happiness.

When after badminton game, we rested on the steps of the college library in the evening, Bhai used to come and entertain us with his Nepalese ethos and experience. His accents of the regional language are very funny to listen to and sometimes we could not follow what he said. Then he would explain it in Hindi. He said that in Nepal he had four acres of land at the town, which valued a hundred thousand rupees per hundredth (of an acre).

The news was astounding to us because he was a millionaire there, far better off than us, and here was just like a servant. He would never sit on the step near us though we invited him. He with all his humility would say that we were big people and he only a peon. He would squat on the floor of the porch.

One day, as we took our seats after playing, Bhai was watering a plant.

"Bhai, what's that plant?" I asked him.

"Sir, it's a mango plant, which I bought from the nursery for Rs. 50. It will remain here in memory of me after I retire from service."

Bhai watered it every day all through the summer. Some days he would draw our attention to it and say, "Sirs, my mango plant is growing fast. Perhaps it may bear fruit before I retire."

Bhai has married twice. His first wife died of some disease, he still doesn't know what. He has four children from her. Bhai used to visit his family once in a year during the summer vacation. As he is a non-vacation staffer, he took his earned leave and casual leaves and spend some one and a half months with his family.

Because a money-order could not be sent to Nepal, he could not send any money to his home when there was any dire necessity. His first wife died since she could not be treated at the proper time. Bhai's eldest son is working as a watchman in another college some sixty kilometres away from our college. With the meagre salary he earned plus some money borrowed from, us Bhai visited his house every year.

Keeping money safe during the train travel (a long five day trip) was highly risky, he used to say. Bhai went home along with one or two friends working in our neighbourhood. When one was sleeping, the other would sit awake. Thousands of rupees were kept in the inner pockets of the undergarment specially stitched for the purpose. Though Bhai had land worth millions of rupees, his family lived in poverty. He was not willing to dispose the property to wipe out poverty. He built a house with a loan taken from the college co-operative society.

One day Bhai came to us in the evening. He was in tears. He took a photo from his pocket and showed it to us.

"Sirs, this is my daughter. She is no more now."

We looked at the photo. It looked like a film star, about seventeen or eighteen years old. Extremely beautiful!

"Bhai, what was her disease?" I enquired.

"Sir, she died last week. I received the letter today. She had some fever, it is written, and she was taking medicine. There aren't good hospitals nearby and who is there to take her to the city hospital, sir?" he was sobbing.

"Didn't they phone you the day she died?"

"Sir, there is no phone facility in our land."

We didn't know how to console him. And who on earth could do that? Bhai with that photo reminded me of Rehman of Tagore's "Kabuliwallah" treasuring his daughter's photo and longing for reunion with her.

After his first wife's death, Bhai married again and has two children from that alliance. They are below the age of ten now. Bhai has only one more year of service left here. We used to ask him what he would do after the retirement. He replied that if his service was needed in our college he would continue here as a guest watchman, ready to serve for Rs. 5000 per month.

Going back to his country would mean sitting idle there. He would get no employment. His wife and children can manage the work on their land. So he longed to continue here after his retirement. Moreover, he has lived in this country since he was sixteen, and he wishes to continue here till he is elderly. In some evenings after an intake of low-priced liquor—his greatest enjoyment—he would come to the campus wavering and try to evade us. Then we would call out to him just to hear his intoxicated talk. The way he controlled his words and how he failed in it was interesting to the ears.

* * *

It was 8 am, Sunday. My telephone rang and I took the cal.

"Hello Sandeep, I am the Principal calling."

"Hello Sir, what's the news?"

"Our Bhai was found dead in his room. Please come soon."

"Oh my God! I am coming."

I rushed to the college and went to the Principal's room. He was not there. I ran to Bhai's room. Bhai's body was found on his bed. He was half naked. The Principal was there along with a few other staff.

"Sir, how did it happen?" I asked the Principal.

"Early morning he got up and appeared before my room with the newspapers. Then he went to the pump house and pumped water to the tank. I rang for him at 7.30 a.m. but he didn't turn up. I tried again after fifteen minutes but he didn't appear. So I went to his room and to my horror found him dead like this. Might be a cardiac arrest."

The police were informed and they came within five minutes. Soon there was a rush of college staff and neighbours. The dead body was taken to the hospital for a post-mortem. The doctor confirmed that it was a cardiac arrest. We couldn't believe that our beloved Bhai was no more with us. The female staff cried.

The Principal declared a holiday for the college on Monday. A condolence meeting was also arranged. Bhai's body, which was kept in the freezer, was brought to the college on Monday at 10 a.m. The students, management representatives and the neighbours swarmed around the body and paid homage to Bhai. Condolence speeches came one after another.

As the body could not be taken to Nepal—it is a hugely expensive thing—it was decided to cremate the body in the municipal crematorium. The only kin who could be consulted was his eldest son, working in a college some sixty kilometres away. He was phoned and he came on Sunday. Bhai's dead body was taken in an ambulance to the crematorium. We all followed it in our cars and hired vehicles. The corpse was taken from the ambulance and placed on the mobile table to be carried to the furnace. With the help of his relatives and friends from Nepal, Bhai's eldest son did the necessary burial rites. Just for five minutes.

The son was crying and tears were flowing from his cheeks. We couldn't bear the sight. I just thought of Bhai's miserable wife and other children who could not see his body and give the final kiss. My eyes were filled with tears. Who would console them? Only one month ago that he'd returned from his home. The warm memories of his stay with them were still in their minds and now they'd have to be frozen and dead. Inexplicable is the grief of that bereaved family! Compared to them, our loss of Bhai is nothing. The corpse was slid to the incinerator and the door was shut. The switch was on and with a horrifying thud the electric incinerator started functioning. LPG from three cylinders was burning

Bhai's body. Smoke appeared thick at the tall chimney. Bhai's soul was going up to heaven. I watched it for some time. After an hour we returned to our houses. Bhai's memory haunted me for several days and disturbed my sleep.

* * *

Oh! The time is 8 p.m. I am all alone there before the college library. I looked at the young mango tree which Bhai had planted three years back. There were bunches of flowers on it. Bhai's eldest son came with Bhai's second wife to our college today to complete formalities of the pension. Some eighteen months have passed since Bhai left us. Yet his pension has not been released to his wife. While I heard Bhai calling me was only a hallucination, I understood. I returned to my house sad and forlorn.

~ ~ ~

10 – Twisted Course of Destiny

Rajiv was a young man in his early thirties, without permanent employment. What he did have was a master's degree in mathematics and he'd passed the NET[5] also. He was taking classes in an entrance coaching centre for Rs. 10,000 per month. His mother, who'd brought him up ,and his younger sister, had been working as day labourers at building construction sites. She is 63 and arthritic. Father died in a bike accident when Rajiv was only ten. He was a barman who never drank. Rajiv's sister, Rema was only two years junior to him and still unmarried. She wasn't studious like Rajiv and had to end her education after pre-degree courses. The pre-university course or pre-degree course, popularly abbreviated to PUC or PDC, is an intermediate course (which is known as 10+2) of two years' duration, conducted by state education institutions or boards in India.

Born of poor dark parents, Rajiv and Rema are not fair in complexion or attractive. Who will marry a lady who is neither fair nor wealthy enough to give any dowry? The dowry has become such a national curse that thousands of women are destined to remain spinsters despised by kith and kin, and society as such. Rajiv's meagre salary met the household expenditure as well as the medicine for his ailing mother. The family lived in a hut built by his father in a 1/33rd of an acre which he had bought with the money he'd earned from the bar.

Rajiv passed his tenth class with 90% of marks at the age of sixteen, and his mother sent him to a college in the town for pre-degree course, taking mathematics, chemistry and physics as the optional subjects. Though it was an additional financial burden to her, the mother dreamt of a bright future when her son would get government employment after education and thus save the family from the abyss of poverty and distress. Rajiv was the most brilliant student in the class and smart in all activities—speech, music, sports and games etc. Naturally, he was chosen

---

[5] NET or National Eligibility Test, is a test to determine eligibility for college and university level lecturership and for the award of Junior Research Fellowship for Indian nationals.

the leader of the class. He was the favourite of the teachers as well as students.

When his classmates of average intelligence attended coaching classes for the entrance examination to the engineering degree program on Saturdays and Sundays, Rajiv had to envy them since he couldn't afford to pay fees for such classes. What use, even if he got a good rank in the entrance exams? His mother wouldn't be able to send him to an engineering college in the city.

Rajiv passed his pre-degree examinations with 88%. He wanted to go for a B.Sc., but his mother couldn't send him as she struggled really hard to sustain the family. As she got a wage of only Rs. 150, there was nothing left for his higher education. Rajiv's thirst for a degree found a means for its accomplishment. There was a tutoring centre in the town providing tutorial classes for high school pupils. Rajiv sought for employment there and since he was brilliant in mathematics, he was appointed. He was offered a monthly salary of Rs. 2,500. With the money he earned thus, he registered as a private candidate for B.Sc. Mathematics course. Teaching and study went simultaneously without any obstacles. Since he was bright enough, he could learn the subjects without the help of any teacher. Years passed very smoothly and he passed B.Sc. examinations with 80%.

What next? The big question mark appeared before Rajiv. In a state like his own (Kerala), mere graduation will not give one government employment. There was no other option for Rajiv than going for an M.Sc. course. Still continuing as a tutor, he registered for M.Sc. Mathematics as a private candidate. Another two years passed and Rajiv became a post-graduate at the 75% level of performance. His post-graduate degree enabled him to get an appointment in a private coaching centre for a medical/engineering entrance test. He was offered a salary of Rs. 5000 per month.

In the coaching centre, physics was handled by Ms. Sangeeta Gopal. She was fair-looking and very gentle in her words and actions. Besides Rajiv and Sangeeta there was a chemistry teacher, Ms. Rohini, a biology teacher, Mr. Madhu, and the Principal, Mr. Murali.

Sangeeta had a special liking for Rajiv. She liked to be with him and talked to him whenever they were free. Which man's heart can be insensitive to the sweet loving looks and expressions? Rajiv for the first time experienced heartthrobs of love and their love grew fast and started to bloom. One day when they were alone in the staff room. Rajiv told

Sangeeta, "Sangeeta, do you love me genuinely? I may not be able to marry you unless I get a permanent job. When it is, I can't say."

"Rajiv, I will wait for you till you get permanent employment. If I marry at all, it will be you and no one else. I have already enthroned you as my husband in my heart and I can't think of anyone else in my life."

"Sangeeta, you are now 23 and your parents will start thinking of your marriage. You are very beautiful and your parents have sufficient wealth to meet the demands of a suitable bridegroom."

"I'll tell my parents that I don't want any marriage now. Let me get a government job first. Thus I can drop their proposals. I don't think they will act against my wishes."

"My mind says, Sangeeta, that you will get a permanent job before I get one. Then how will you resist your parents' proposals?"

"I will tell them then that I am in love with you and I would only marry you. Rajiv, this is my promise. Kindly stretch your palm." He stretched his right palm and she pressed hers on it.

"Sangeeta, I will wait for you and we will live together forever."

Their golden moments ended when the bell was rung and the other colleagues entered into the staff room.

Rajiv started to dream of a happy married life with Sangeeta. Its fulfilment required a permanent job. His ambition was to become a college lecturer. He knew very well that this was a herculean task to get such an appointment. He couldn't expect it in government aided private colleges, since they demanded a high donation. He could try for it only in government colleges, which were very few in number. He decided to sit for the University Grants Commission (UGC) National Eligibility Test (NET) examination which is the eligibility for applying for the post. He cleared the NET exams at the first attempt. As the state was going through a great financial crisis, the government banned all appointments and the Public Service Commission stopped notifications.

Life's road is never smooth and straight. It has to climb hilly roads full of sharp curves before coming down again to the plains. Rajiv's life has been passing through the easy straight roads and the time had come for him to climb the hill before him. His mother, who had been the main bread earner of the family, started to show the symptom of arthritis. The severe pain in her joints prevented her from heavy work, and she was compelled to stop her sustaining job of a day labourer. Rajiv's sister, Rema, somehow passed her pre-degree course on the third try. She couldn't be sent for higher education, and hence remained in the house, helping her sick mother in domestic activities. The sole responsibility and burden of maintaining the family rested on Rajiv. With a monthly salary of Rs. 6000, he had to meet the domestic expenses and mother's treatment charges.

Years passed one after another. The new government which came into power after the general elections lifted the ban on government employment, and Rajiv applied for every post he was eligible for—from lowest grade to that of college lecturer. The Public Service Commission's test, interview and appointment go at a snail's pace, taking several years. Domestic worries, agonies and tensions of Rajiv were subdued and relieved by the caressing touch of Sangeeta's love in the coaching centre. She too applied for government jobs through PSC. Both attempted several tests and waited for the results.

One day when Rajiv and Sangeeta were sharing their domestic news, the postman appeared with a letter for Sangeeta. It was an advice memo from PSC, asking her to join the Education Department as a Lower Division Clerk. Sangeeta was highly elated. Rajiv had also sat for the same examination, but luck was against him. Sangeeta belonged to Other Backward Community, which has reservations in government employment. Though Rajiv was financially poor he belonged to the forward community, and this denied him any special privilege.

"Sangeeta, my hearty congrats! We should celebrate it," Rajiv said.

"Thanks, dear Rajiv. It's surprising why you are not selected. How much brighter you are! Maybe you will be called later from the list."

"God knows. Let Him guide me as He wills. Which is the joining date?"

"Before the 20th of this month. Only fifteen days more."

"It's better to join at the earliest. I mean tomorrow itself."

"My only pain is to leave you, Rajiv. The District Education Office where I have to go is far away. Anyway we will be in touch over the phone."

"Don't worry, Sangeeta. We'll be in touch. My only request is that you should not forget me when you enter into a new world and new acquaintances."

"Don't speak such rubbish, dear Rajiv. How can I forget you? You will always be in my mind."

"Your parents will insist for your marriage as you are already 26 now. How will you resist it?"

"Didn't I promise you that I will not marry anyone else? I will tell my parents about our love and request them to wait for your permanent employment."

"But how long can they wait? How unfortunate I am!"

"Don't be pessimistic, dear Rajiv. We shall pray to God to unite us at the earliest."

"Ok dear. You may join tomorrow. Let's stop. Others are coming."

They ended their conversation. Sangeeta disclosed the news of her selection to the other colleagues and the principal arranged a farewell meeting. The love between Sangeeta and Rajiv was unknown to others. Both could control their emotions in the presence of others. But when Rajiv spoke at the meeting, his voice choked. He struggled hard to appear calm. The lovers' parting at 4 pm after the classes let out was really in tears. They waited for the others to leave the campus.

"Sangeeta, we never thought that we'd have to part so soon. We've been here so close together for three years. In fact, you have been the north star who guided me when I have been swaying in the tempest of grief. What will I do when you are gone?"

"Rajiv, the north star is always there and nothing can hide it from you. I will be in regular touch with you and we can meet at the park on Sundays. I plan to come every weekend."

"You can't measure my love for you. Who can measure the quantity of water in the ocean? Or its depth? My mind can't go on thinking without you even for an hour. Then how can I remain without you for a week?"

"Rajiv, don't drown me in that ocean of passion. Do you think my love for you is not that deep as yours? Do you think I will be happy without you?" Tears started flowing over her rosy cheeks.

"Oh, don't cry, my darling. I know how much you love me." He wiped away her tears with his hand and gave a kiss on her forehead. "We should not be sentimental like teenagers. We have to be practical. Cheer up now."

"Papa will be accompanying me tomorrow. I will seek boarding in the working women's hostel. I will call you next evening. "

"OK, dear. You may go now. Best wishes!"

"Thanks, dear Rajiv. Best wishes to you! I will always pray for your employment and our life together." Thus they departed.

Needless to say, Rajiv was most upset, drowned in grief as his north star left him. Sangeeta called him the next evening and detailed her new world. She was no doubt content with her new atmosphere. Both of them phoned almost every evening. As promised, Sangeeta met him at the park next Sunday. She was full of gossip about her colleagues, hostel mates, office work etc.

Rajiv got an alarming phone call from her on Monday evening. Her parents had found a suitable match for her. The boy was her father's friend's son, a teacher in a higher secondary school. She expressed her dissent and had to tell her parents of her love for Rajiv. The parents became very furious and said that they would never allow her to marry him, because he had no permanent employment. Sangeeta was really upset and told him that she was willing to elope with him and get a registered marriage if he could save her.

Lightning shot through Rajiv's heart. Fortunately his sense conquered the emotions, and he could think very practically. It would be cruellest of her to disobey her parents and push them to the abyss of sorrow and dejection. Rajiv advised her not to displease her parents, and agree to the marriage. She couldn't agree to his advice first, but he convinced her that there was no other option before them. He told her not to call him any more so that they could forget each other, which was what the situation demanded. Even though he was invited for the wedding he didn't attend because, he couldn't bear the sight of another person having her as a life partner.

Rajiv continued his teaching in the coaching centre. He wanted to escape from the morose atmosphere there. He tried to forget Sangeeta by reading more. He was writing exam after exam for the Public Service Commission, Banking Service Recruitment Board, etc. But luck was against him and the appointment eluded him. He had now completed four years of service in the coaching centre and was getting Rs. 10,000 per month, whereas a lowest grade employee of a government office drew a starting salary of Rs. 13,000.

Finally, Rajiv's prayers were granted and he got appointment as a peon in the District Collector's Office. A postgraduate has to work as a peon! Something is better than nothing, he consoled himself. He joined the office, which was sixty kilometres away from his house. The majority of his superior officers in the office—clerks, superintendents, accounts officer, were all inferior to him in education—passed only tenth class, pre degree or degree. They were sympathetic to him, but superiors are always superiors and he had to obey their commands, fetching files and serving them from section to section. His thirst for higher education and a better job prompted him to do a Ph.D. as a part-time scholar. Fortunately, his college classmate, Dr Joseph, was a research guide in an aided college in the town. Rajiv stayed in a lodge near his office and went home every weekend. The monotony and humiliation of his peon work was compensated by the research activities. He use all his vacation time to visit the research centre. He completed the required attendances and submitted the thesis after three years. The evaluation took only three months and he was awarded PhD at the age of 34.

One day as part of his routine duty, Rajiv was asked by the senior superintendent to serve a file to the Deputy Collector who took charge on that day. He was benumbed by the sight of the Deputy Collector. She looked very much like his Sangeeta. But how could she be here? True, it was she herself because the name board on the table read Sangeeta Gopal.

"Good morning, madam!" He put the file on the table before her.

"Good morning!" She looked on his face and exclaimed, "You are Rajiv!"

"Yes madam. I am that unfortunate Rajiv."

"What a pity! You couldn't get a better job?"

"No madam. I got this appointment only three years back. I have taken many other tests, but luck is against me."

"Don't be dejected, Rajiv. I sat for the Deputy Collector examinations and got this appointment. You too can apply that way. What about your wife and children?"

"I am still a bachelor, madam. Not planning for a marriage now."

"OK, I shall pray for you, Rajiv. God will save you, no doubt, rewarding your goodness. You may go now."

Rajiv went back to his seat. How he could muster strength and energy in front of Sangeeta remained strange. *My God, what a test it is!* His mind was throbbing with great agony. At the same time, he experienced some hidden pleasure lurking in some corner of his mind—the pleasure of meeting his former beloved after seven years! He had no jealousy of her, even if she had a superior job, because his passion for her was so great.

But facing her as another man's wife and his superior *boss* was intolerable to him. His conscience told him that it was a sin to look at Sangeeta as his earlier lover. He found it very difficult to see her as another man's wife. But what to do now except accept the stark reality? If God wants him to undergo further trials, let His will be done, Rajiv pacified his mind.

With a dispassionate mechanical mind, Rajiv continued his office work. Three months passed. One evening he got a phone call from his home.

"Hello Rema! What's the news?"

"Happy news, brother! You have got an advice memo from the PSC requesting you to join as Assistant Professor of Mathematics in Maharajas Government College, Kochi. "

"Oh my God, what a surprise, thrilling news! I am coming home tomorrow."

Thus God granted Rajiv's prayers at last. Maybe Sangeeta's as well.

~ ~ ~

11 – Puppets in the Hands of God

As usual, I was sauntering to the town in the evening. Being Christmas Day, the shops were shut and the road was having less traffic. Themes for my poems and short stories are moulded and developed during these walks in the evenings and mornings. Occasionally, I get new themes or plots from the sights and incidents I view on my stroll. As I reached in front of the hardware shop, the security person who used to greet me was missing. Perhaps, he went to his house to celebrate Christmas with his family, I thought. Even though we used to greet each other, I hadn't asked his name or where he came from. He looked pretty old, weak, grey-haired man, and might have been in his late sixties or early seventies. Seeing him, very often I thought about the sad plight of my state of Kerala as well as the nation of India itself.

Suddenly, I heard a gasping sound from the right side-yard of the shop. It was nightfall and I had to search for the source of the sound. I found the security man lying flat. I asked him, "*Chettan* (elder brother), what happened to you?"

The answer was a low murmur: "Sir, please take me to hospital, or I may die."

Fortunately an auto rickshaw passed on the road and I told the driver that we should take the man to the hospital. He was admitted to the casualty section and the doctor asked the nurse to give him a high dose of insulin. After some fifteen minutes, the patient's condition improved. Since he was very weak, the doctor said that he should stay in the hospital for a few days. When I told the doctor that I was only an acquaintance and not a relative of the patient, he asked me to inform the family of the security man. I paid the bill for the treatment already done. He was taken to a general ward and I accompanied him.

When he was in a position to speak I asked him, "Chettan, what's your name and where is your house?"

"Sir, I am Krishnan Nair and I live in a village far away in the high ranges, called Chemmannar."

"You have to stay in the hospital under medication for a few days, the doctor has said. We have to inform your family and someone should stay with you as a caregiver."

The reply was a deep sigh, and in a wailing tone he said, "I have no one in the house to stay with me, sir. My daughter-in-law and her two little daughters are my sole family members. The monthly salary of Rs. 6000 I get from my security job is the only income that maintains them. We are living in a rented hut, paying Rs. 1000 as rent per month. Sir, I should have lived comfortably like you, but the fate has been cruel to me. Why? I don't know. I haven't done any wrong to any person. As far as possible I have been leading a *sattvika* (selfless, compassionate and serviceable to others) life. Then why is God so cruel to me? Why is He so cruel to my daughter-in-law and the little angel-like daughters? Might be, punishment for the sins of our earlier births."

"Chettan, kindly explain what happened to you. I would like to hear of your past." My hidden interest of getting a plot for a short story prompted me to speak so.

"I belong to a rich Nair hereditary family. I had my childhood with my parents and six siblings at Kottayam. Our family was one of the richest in the locality. Characteristic of the Nair caste, my parents were lazy people and earned nothing, but spent what they had inherited.

"We had some fifteen acres of land, of which half remained fallow. The rest were given to lessees who worked in our lands and gave us a share of their harvest. No doubt there was exploitation from their part, but we shall not blame them since we were not prepared to work or supervise what they had been doing. Ownership of some portion of our land went to the tenants as part of the land reform act of the government and we had only ten acres left for our possession.

"Our parents did not educate us much, since fees had to be paid in college and thus we had all to end our study after 10th grade. We were asked to work on the land, but like our parents, we too were indolent. Reluctantly, we were compelled to turn to agriculture.

"One after another, my elder brothers got married and our only sister was married off. My parents compelled me to marry when I entered my twenty-eighth year. Thus, I, the youngest of the family, got married to a Nair caste lady belonging to a middle income family. The ancestral property was divided among us, and each had a share of one acre. My elder brothers made small houses on their property and maintained their family somehow, working their land." He seemed tired of talking.

"Kindly have a break now and drink some water." I gave him a glass of water. When he finished drinking I asked him to continue.

"Sir, before continuing, kindly request the doctor to discharge me, because I have no money to pay the bills and there is no one to stay with me in the hospital. I have only some Rs. 100 with me. I gave my last month's salary to the daughter-in-law when I went home last week. I think that I can regain my health if I take rest at home. The majority of doctors nowadays are greedy in that they want to exploit the patients for maximum fees. I have been a diabetic patient for several years and have been taking insulin for it. Unfortunately, since the nearest hotel was closed today, I couldn't take my lunch. That's why I collapsed."

"Chettan, don't worry about the treatment charges. I will pay for you. Moreover, I will ask my driver to stay with you in the hospital. I will speak to the doctor and request him to discharge you at the earliest. Now, let me hear the rest of your life history."

"I don't know how to thank you, Sir. God bless you for the service you are rendering to this poor old man. Let me continue. My wife, Lakshmi, was weak in her health and after ten years of marriage, she had only she gave birth to our only son, and that following lengthy fertility treatments. The doctor who treated her warned us that she was not healthy enough to conceive again. We three stayed with our parents for nearly ten years. Since the income from our one acre of our land was so small, my wife suggested to me, "Why don't we sell this property and buy more land in the high ranges and stay there? Our son is to be given good education and we need more income. If the parents are coming with us, let them come, or let them stay with one of our brothers, and the parents' property shall be given to him."

"That's a good idea, dear Lakshmi. I shall consult with the parents and the brothers," I told her.

"Even though my parents and brothers objected to our plan initially, they gave us permission to leave them. My eldest brother decided to buy my property as well as the parents', and look after the parents in his house. Thus I got Rs. 300,000 for our land and with that we bought five acres at Chemmannar, near to the border of Tamil Nadu State. There was a small tiled house on the plot as well. Cardamom and pepper were the main yield of the land. Life went very smoothly.

After finishing the 10th class, our son Arvind was sent for aPre-Degree Course (PDC) and along with it coaching for the engineering entrance test. He passed PDC with 80% of marks and also passed the college entrance test. He got admission for Bachelors of Technology in the Government College of Engineering and Technology at Kochi. After four years, he completed his engineering course in Information Technology. He didn't study well, and as a result he got only a second class.

Since job opportunities were less and engineering graduates were innumerable in Kerala, a master's degree was the minimum needed for a job in the IT sector. Arvind's marks were too low for admission. Sir, you can imagine the dejection of an unemployed youth. He was not prepared to work the land and insisted that he should start a business of his own.

Meanwhile my wife Lakshmi showed symptoms of cancer in her stomach. Several hundred thousand rupees had to be spent for her treatment, and I was compelled to sell two acres of land for it. Most unfortunately, after six months of continuous treatment, she departed." Telling this he started crying like a child. I tried to pacify his grief in vain. My eyes also welled.

After five minutes he continued, "Two months before her death she told me:

"Dear, I may die at any time. Who is there to look after you and our Arvind? You are only fifty-eight now. You should marry another lady after my death. Arvind has been insisting on starting a business of his own. Since the government will grant loans for self-employment, kindly yield to his wish. We will have to pledge our land, but we can close the loan within five years. Moreover, you too can supervise his business and it will not run to loss."

"Lakshmi, don't be so negative and pessimistic. We are all praying to God and He will grant our prayers and you will live long. Kindly don't speak of my second marriage. I can never place another lady in my mind. I love you so much, and it will remain so till my death. I will look after Arvind if anything happens to you. I am healthy enough to do the cooking and other activities. As it is your desire, we shall pledge the land and take loan for his business."

Thus our landed property of three acres was pledged in a nationalized bank for a loan of Rs. 500,000, and Arvind opened an internet café cum publishing-and-photocopy centre in the town of Nedumkandam. A large room was rented and furnished it with several computers, Xerox machines and other needed furniture. Two staff were appointed. Arvind was no doubt very happy. He bought a bike and rode to the café daily. Though customers were few in the initial days, gradually the business went without any loss. Lakshmi's condition became worse and she departed us, leaving me in an ocean of grief. After her death, I had to do all the kitchen work in the morning and then do farming till the evening. Arvind went to the café at 8 am and returned only at 9 pm.

Months and years passed one after another, and Arvind's conduct showed changes. It seemed that he had fallen into the clutches of bad companions and returned home very late. He would be drunk and never took any food from the house. He paid deaf ears to my advice. I thought that he would improve if he married a good natured girl. Though he objected at first to my request, he finally agreed to marry. Thus he was married to a pretty girl, although not getting any dowry. Both Arvind and I were against the dowry system and we didn't demand anything. It seemed that marriage changed his character. He was very loving to his wife Ratnam and after a year a girl was born to them.

The happiness of the family didn't last long. Arvind fell into the trap of bad companions again. He used to come home late drunk, and there were days even when he never make it home. Since he was going on his bike, it was a cause of tension for me and Ratnam. Then one day I received a registered notice from the bank asking me to remit Rs. 1,000,000 as loan capital and interest within a month. If not done, the landed property which we had pledged for the loan would be confiscated by the court.

I had been under the impression that Arvind had been repaying the loan by instalments, for once when I enquired him about it he told me that he had been regularly repaying the loan without any default. The notice was a heavy shock to me like a lightning passing through my heart. Meanwhile, Ratnam was seven months pregnant.

When Arvind returned home that night, drunk as usual, I had to quarrel with him and he suddenly went out of the house on his bike. He didn't come back, Sir." Krishnan Nair started crying again. "The morning broke with an ambulance carrying his dead body home, Sir," he was sobbing.

"Ratnam fell unconscious and was admitted to hospital. After a month, the bank appropriated our property and I had to leave my house, taking Ratnam and her daughter to a rented house. Ratnam gave birth to another daughter, who is now two years old.

"I, who have become diabetic, had to find a means for looking after the family, and thus I am here, Sir, as a security person." He started coughing, rubbing his chest with right hand. His head was stooping down and I guessed that he was collapsing. I propped him quickly and laid him on the bed. Â I called loudly for the help of the doctor.

The nurses rushed in and immediately he was taken to the intensive care unit. I too followed them. The doctor made check-ups and supplied him oxygen. The doctor said in a low voice that the patient had a cardiac arrest and he was dead already. He scolded me for allowing the patient to speak so much that made his condition worse.

I was terribly upset. My conscience told me that I had killed Krishnan Nair. Immediately I phoned my wife and said that I had to take the dead body of Krishnan Nair to his house at Chemmannar and would return home only the next day after the burial. My wife might have thought that I had become mad. I didn't tell her that I was responsible for the immediate death of Krishnan Nair.

I booked an ambulance and took the body of Krishnan Nair into it with the help of the hospital staff. I was travelling all alone with the dead body. There was only the driver as company for me. How would I face Ratnam, waking her up at this late night carrying her father-in-law's dead body? I started thinking. The body would reach there only after midnight.

Reaching Chemmannar, I sought the help of the police. Two constables were sent to accompany me, and the dead body was brought to the house. Ratnam couldn't bear the sight and started wailing, beating on her breast. Her sobbing words "who will look after us?" went like an arrow through my mind.

Meanwhile some neighbours also reached the house. Krishnan Nair's relatives were informed by phone. The next day, the body was cremated at the public crematorium. Now the question remained—who would look after Ratnam and her children? My mind didn't allow me to leave the family deserted. Moreover, I was to some extend responsible for the family's present plight.

Before leaving, I gave Ratnam Rs. 5000 and told her, "Keep this with you. I will request one of my friends who has a tea factory at Peermade to give you the job of an office assistant there. There you will get good salary and free quarters to live." She thanked me with clasped hands. Thus I made penance for the inadvertent crime I have committed, by securing Ratnam a comfortable life. She was appointed in the factory after a week. The tragedy of Krishnan Nair and his family confirmed the adage that we are all puppets in the hands of God.

~ ~ ~

12 – Burn Your Horoscope!

Praveen is a smart electronic engineer at Wipro. He is very handsome, affable and conquers minds through his ever-smiling face. He wins respect from his superiors as well as subordinates through commitment to his profession. But one problem is bothering him, his parents and kith and kin. Though aged thirty-five, he remains still a bachelor. It's none of his fault that he remains single. He has been seeking a life partner for the past eight years. His parents are more worried than he is. His only sibling, a younger sister, was married off ten years ago, and has two children studying in school.

Praveen's villain is his horoscope. He is a Brahmin and his parents are highly orthodox. They have blind belief in the power of the horoscope. Praveen's horoscope predicts that he is unlikely to have a long married life—his wife will die within one year of his marriage. Innumerable proposals have come from different quarters, from good-looking, well-employed girls. They all withdrew when they read his horoscope. Which girl would risk death by marrying him? Which parent would send his/her daughter to the gallows?

In fact Praveen has no belief in the horoscope. He believes that stars and planets are just creations of God as human beings and other things are. So they can't be any determining factor to other creations' destiny. It's ultimately the Creator who decides what one should be. Being highly obedient and loving his parents so much, he could not fall in love with any girl who was rational like him.

One evening Praveen told his dad, "Dad, let me advertise in the matrimonial page of *The Hindu*?"

"What use? The girl's parents will ask for your horoscope," dad replied.

"We shall include the horoscopic prediction in the advertisement," he suggested.

"Right. If any girl or parents are willing, let them reply," ma replied.

"OK, you may do so. I don't think anybody will turn up," dad said. Praveen drafted the advertisement. It read so:

BRIDE NEEDED

Praveen, Brahmin youth aged 35, handsome, 6 feet, working in Wipro, Bangalore as electronics engineer needs good looking, employed bride. Horoscope predicts wife's death within a year. Interested girls and parents may contact: praveenwipro@gmail.com

The matrimonial was handed over to the newspaper office along with the advertisement charge.

Sunday morning. Praveen looked into *The Hindu* to see his matrimonial. It was there without any spelling mistake or typo errors. Having read it he couldn't suppress his laugh. "Which fool will come forward?" his inner voice asked him. He just went through the other matrimonials. Nothing strange or funny in them! Suddenly his eyes locked at an advertisement:

BRIDEGROOM NEEDED

Parvati, Brahmin lady aged 30, good looking, postgraduate in English, 5 feet 8 inches, working as guest lecturer, needs well employed bridegroom. No barrier on caste. Horoscopic alert: husband may die within six months. Those interested may contact: krishnarj007@gmail.com

"Hurrah! Parvati may be my life partner," Praveen jumped up and exclaimed.

"Praveen, what's wrong with you?" ma asked.

"Ma kindly look at this matrimonial. This is our matrimonial and this one a similar one from one Parvati," Praveen pointed them out.

"My God, we don't want her. If the prediction comes true . . . Even if you remain single we need you always with us," Ma cried.

Hearing them talk, dad came from his office.

"Has our matrimonial come in the paper?" he enquired.

Praveen showed him both the matrimonials.

"Very strange and coincidental! Are you interested in her proposal?" dad asked.

"Yes dad. I am going to write to her," Praveen replied.

"What? If anything happens to you?" Dad asked.

"Dear dad and ma, the Creator has decided what we ought to be. Just surrender to His will and pleasure. I have waited all these years for a match. My damned horoscope dissuaded all proposers. I have told you several times that I have no belief in it. It's all because of your obstinacy that I couldn't search for a rational girl. This lady belongs to our same caste. It seems that she has no belief in a horoscope and may accept my proposal. So, if she is willing I will marry her. You may kindly allow me to propose to her," Praveen implored.

"OK, son, if you insist so, we won't object to it. Let things happen as God wills," dad replied.

Praveen sent an email to Parvati detailing his status, horoscopic prediction and willingness to marry her. He asked her to reply, detailing her whereabouts. Parvati was only too happy to have him as her husband, for she, like him believed that horoscope was a means of the religious mafia to exploit the laity. She wrote a long mail to Praveen expressing her willingness as well as detailing her bio data. She was the only daughter of her parents who were doctors practising in their own hospital. Although she had a postgraduate degree in English, she couldn't get a regular appointment as lecturer since the State government had banned appointments for several years.

The marriage date was fixed. 10th November at the nearby temple. Praveen wedded Parvati in the presence of a small gathering of close relatives and friends. The entire gathering, well aware of the couples' horoscopic prediction, prayed intensely to the gods to avert their future catastrophe. Needless to say, neither Praveen and Parvaty worried at all during the marriage ceremony, during the first night, or the honeymoon days that followed.

To the amazement of all, the gift raffle ticket which Parvati got from the jewellery shop when she bought the wedding ornaments won first prize of one kilogram of gold on the draw date of first December. Four months after their marriage, another fortune embraced them. Parvati got a permanent appointment in a government college as lecturer in English. Their happy days went one after another. Five months... six months... Nothing happened to Praveen. He got promotion as executive engineer. One year passed... nothing happened to Parvati except that she became pregnant. They celebrated their first wedding anniversary by burning their horoscope papers like a campfire to the mirth of their parents gathered on the front yard. The parents now understood the folly of horoscopes and how innocent people are cheated by astrologers supported by priests.

Parvaty gave birth to a cute son. Five years passed...

Parvaty delivered a lovely girl.... The wheel of time passed year after year... ten years... twenty years... twenty-five years.

Praveen and Parvati are celebrating their silver wedding jubilee today. Their son Prasanth and daughter Pallavi have arranged a feast in their house to felicitate the best parents in the world. Relatives, friends and neighbours were invited for the function. Parents of both Praveen and Parvati had already bidden adieu to the world, content of their children's happy married life.

When felicitations were over, Praveen got up to express their gratitude to all. In his brief speech, he narrated their bitter days of fighting with their horoscopes before the marriage. He wound up his speech thus: "I exhort you, my good friends, neighbours, relatives and younger generation: you should burn your horoscope. Then success is yours."

~ ~ ~

13 – Ammu's Birthday

"Tomorrow is 19th November, and my Ammu's fourth birthday. And two days later, on 21st is the seventh birthday of my Anagha." Asha ruminated on how their birthdays had been celebrated splendidly last year when her husband was with them. God was cruel enough to call him back, leaving these two kids on her shoulders. She now has to work hard as a day labourer for the sustenance of the family. She has to look after her mother also. Her husband Laxman had indeed been a yacht to her and the kids, and they knew no worries and enjoyed voyaging from shore to shore of pleasures and happiness. He was run over by a car one evening as he was returning from the factory on his bike.

"Dear, I don't have any money to celebrate our daughters' birthdays separately as you have done in the previous years," Asha whispered, looking at her husband's photo. In previous years, the relatives as well as close neighbours were invited for the dinner. And amid the jubilant crowd, Anagha and Ammu, wearing dazzling, costly dresses, lit birthday candles to the accompaniment of "Happy birthday to you…" and then cut the cakes and served them to everyone. The kids were given birthday gifts. How they went with those treasures to their bedrooms and how elated they were when they took out the contents! Gone were those golden days. "Dear darling, let there be a minimum celebration at least. Buy new dresses for them and let them be happy tomorrow," her husband seemed to tell her. Asha decided to celebrate the kids' birthdays together, bringing them new dresses, as her husband wished.

"Ma, tomorrow is Ammu's birthday. And on Tuesday, Anagha's. We shall celebrate the days together tomorrow. Let me go to the dress mart to buy new churidars for them. Though your son is gone, we have to at least celebrate the birthdays in a minimal manner," Asha told her mother-in-law.

"True, my daughter. Had he been alive, how jolly would have been the house tomorrow! Asha, have you got money to buy dresses for the kids?"

"Yes ma, I have saved up some money for the purpose."

"Mummy, let me also come to the shop," Ammu cried.

"No Ammu. You may go with grandma to collect some flowers for tomorrow. Ma, get some flowers from our neighbour, Rahim's meadow. You will get bluebells and daisies there."

"OK, daughter. You may go now or you won't get back before dark."

Asha walked along the road to the town. The gentle breeze and the chirping of the birds seemed to her to wish happy birthday to Ammu and Anagha. She entered a small textile shop, looking for a cheap dress. She selected a churidar each for the daughters. The stuff was not that good, for she has only two hundred rupees with her.

"What's the price of these?"

"Three hundred and fifty rupees."

"I have only two hundred rupees with me. Kindly show me cheaper churidars." It was better that she had not brought the daughters or they would have cried for more attractive dresses. She selected two churidars that were within her budget. The kids may not like them much, for their papa bought for them elegant dresses in the previous years. "They would understand our wretched position," she thought. Asha bought half a kilo cake from a bakery to be cut my Ammu and Anagha, the next day. She also bought some candles.

She hurried along the road. The sun has been bidding adieu to the day and the moon peeped from the eastern sky. She reached her house and the front door was open. Inside, Asha found no one. *Hasn't ma come back with the flowers?* she thought. She called loudly, "Ma... Ammu... Anagha..." No reply. She went to her neighbour's, Ravi's house. Only Ravi's ten year old daughter was there.

"Mini, do you know where my Ammu, Anagha and Matha have gone?"

"Auntie, Ammu is missing. All have gone to the river bank in search of her." "My darling Ammu... Where are you?" yelling she flew to the direction of the river.

The entire neighbourhood thronged at the river bank. Seeing the crowd, Asha screamed, "My Ammu, what happened to you?" Her shriek was echoed from the nearby hill and the birds re-echoed it to every nook and corner of the village and to the sky so that Ammu should respond to her mother's call. But there was no reply from Ammu.

"Ma where is our Ammu? Tell me," Asha asked her Ma.

With choking voice, and tears running like rivers, Ma said, "As there were no flowers in Rahim's meadow, we came over here. Telling Ammu to sit here, I and Anagha went there on the riverbed to pluck some flowers.

When we returned, Ammu wasn't found here. We searched for her everywhere... and then informed our neighbours."

The neighbours told her that they had searched for Ammu everywhere, and even in the water. Some of them were found still in the river diving and searching.

"Mummy, where has our Ammu... gone?" Anagha continued, crying, hugging her Ma. "Ammu, here is your birthday churidar. Here is the cake for you. Come my darling... Take them, darling..."

Asha became almost hysterical and threw the dress and cake to the river. The neighbours tried to console her. But who can console a mother who has lost her darling child? She was beating her chest and crying. Was Ammu called back by her papa to heaven? Was he celebrating her first birthday there?

"Dear students, what do you say about this story?" English Professor, Dr. Sankar asked his degree students after reading the entire story in the class room.

"Who wrote this story, sir? Just an ordinary one," Joseph responded.

"What moral is there in this story, sir? We are fed up with reading such tragic incidents in the newspapers," Meera exclaimed.

"What Meera said is true, sir. We need to hear something merry and pleasant. The very life is full of miseries and sorrows. So we ought to seek something good-humoured," the philosophic Hari emphasised.

"What justification is there in the tragedy of Ammu, sir? She was an angel who hasn't committed a sin in her life. Yet she was called back by the Creator. Is the Creator a sadist?" the leftist Abdul retorted.

"Any more comments?" Dr. Sankar asked.

There was no more response from the students.

"My dear students, I honour your reactions. What Joseph said is true. This is just an ordinary story. I am not revealing the author's name. And what relevance has an author in a work as per New Criticism? The author has mentioned as a footnote that the story is based on a tragedy at a village in North Kerala. As Meera has complained, we read such tragic news every day. Dear students, don't forget the fact that our sweetest songs are those that tell of saddest thoughts, as Shelley has written. The more we read such things, the more compassionate and humane we should become. Such literature purges our mind and we get *karunyam* (compassion) rasa.

"We should not turn our faces away from the miseries and tragedies of others. Such tragedies are part of the flow of the system and as participatory beings we should flow with it. Mysterious are the ways of the Creator and our little intelligence can't find justifications for the multitudinous activities of the Almighty. I hope you are satisfied with my answers," Dr. Sankar ended his lecture.

"Yes Sir. Thank you very much," the class responded.

~ ~ ~

14 – Sanchita Karma*

"Why are you so cruel to us, chasing us for such a long time, but not catching us?" the male mouse asked the herd of seven cats, large and small.

"We shall tell you the reason. We are souls of the seven cats whom you poisoned to death in your previous life. Do you know who you were in your last birth? You were Stephen, an Advocate and this, your wife, Stella, a housewife. I am Preethi, the grandma of all these children and grand-children. These two are my first daughters, Manikutty and Ammini. The others are their children, Kinganan, Rowdy, Kittu and Kitty. Tell us why you killed us? What harm did we do to you?" Preethi exploded.

"We don't think that we had a life before this," the male mouse said.

"Even if we had one, we hadn't killed anyone," the female mouse added.

"That's the problem with you. Your religion then had not taught you of the phenomenon of rebirths. You believed that after your death your soul would go either to heaven or hell. You believed in the shallow philosophy that man is the centre of universe and all other creatures are created for you. You believed that you are created in the image of God and you are His favourite. You can't remember your past since divinity has got lost in you by your unholy, criminal deeds," Preethy said.

"We don't understand anything. Kindly tell us what we did in our past," the male mouse said.

"I will take you back to your past. As I said, you were then Stephen, an Advocate who lived with your wife, Stella, in a big mansion-like house in a vast compound. You had two daughters who had professional employment and were, married, and settled in metro cities. You had no domestic animals, not even dogs or cats. You had a neighbour, one Agricultural Officer named Krishnan who lived with his aged mother, employed wife and two children. Being Hindus, Krishnan's family had a culture distinct from yours. They were vegetarians and believed in the philosophy of Advaita. They were our masters who loved us as their own children. We three generations lived with them for five years," Preethy broke for a minute.

"Then what happened?" the female mouse asked.

"Krishnan was also a poet. The poet in him moulded him and his family as nature lovers. He had only 1/10th acre of land and there he planted papaya trees, not for himself or his family, but for birds like crows, mynahs and cuckoos to feast upon the ripe fruits. He fed crows with rice every day, and kept a basin full of water for the birds to drink and bathe.

For us cats, he brought salmon every day when he returned after his morning walk. Thus we were fed with rice and fresh fish. They never allowed us to be hungry even for an hour. We belonged to the Ootty pedigree with bushy tail and snow-white fur. They took us like angels and loved like anything. Krishnan bought plastic balls for us and we enjoyed playing soccer in his drawing and dining rooms. Inexpressible was the happiness the Krishnan family got from our presence there. We sat on their laps, longing for strokes which we got in abundance. Very often, we slept on their sofa and settees which they liked most. Their guests had to sit elsewhere when we occupied their settee," Preethy stopped.

"Then why were you killed by Stephen?" the male mouse asked.

"We cats have no boundaries as you mice do. The Creator has created this earth for all animals and plants. He has not given human beings any special right to fence any land. But the selfish man does so. The divine universal instincts in us tempt us to step over or jump over the boundaries humans make. Thus we lovers of freedom liked to run and play in the vast compound of Stephen. There were great beauties in his compound that attracted us—butterflies, birds, squirrels, grasshoppers and the like. Most of the daytime, we preferred to play there, often running after another in great delight. Stephen and his wife didn't like our presence there. Their petty sense of ownership couldn't tolerate us intruding into their property. Moreover we defecated in the compound, but covered the shit with soil," Preethy stopped for a breath.

"Then you might have entered into his house, which provoked Stephen," the female mouse remarked.

"No. We never did. We never wanted any food since we were well fed by our masters. Stephen might not have liked us defecating in his compound. The paradox is that he and his wife went to church every day. Listened to Christ's message that you have to love your neighbour and even your enemy. Loving your neighbour includes loving whatever possessions and properties your neighbour has. Stephen knew very well that Krishnan and his family loved their cats as their children.

But the devil in him and his wife nurtured hate for us and it ended in poisoning us. Very early morning before going to church, he put some rat poison in fried fish and placed it very close to my master's compound. Which cat is averse to fish? Early morning, when we went out from the master's house, we smelt the tempting aroma of fish and ate the pieces one after another. We were murdered in three attempts. My Manikutty and Ammini were the first victims. How much our masters shed tears then! They didn't complain to Stephen because he would deny it and insult them in return.

Several months after, Kinganan, Rowdy, Kittu and myself were the victims. Our mistress went to Stephen's house then and complained in tears. But they denied the charges and pretended innocence. How my master dug graves for us with aching heart and shaky hands! The poison's effect chased us to our master's kitchen for water, but we couldn't drink. In great distress, wailing, my master and mistress tried to drop water into our mouth with a filler, but we couldn't drink and after several minutes of great pain, shrieking, we bade goodbye to our masters.

After a few months our kitty, just three months old, was also poisoned in the same manner. It was beyond any tolerance for our masters and they decided not to have any more cats in their house in the future. Now you are that Stephen and you, his wife. The cruelty you had shown to us and our masters are the karmas which demanded reaction. The gravity of your crimes was such that it could not be atoned by any punishment when you were still alive as human beings. So, you were destined to be born as mice to be chased by the souls of the seven cats you dispatched in your last birth," Preethy exploded.

"We don't want to live any more. We want Moksha.**

Kindly kill us as we killed you," both the mice implored.

"We never wanted to do so, but the Almighty orders us to dispatch you. It's nothing but Sanchita Karma. My children, finish them now," Preethi ordered and in a few minutes the mice were killed and eaten.

~ ~ ~

❖ *Sanchita Karma* is one of the three Karmas or actions of human beings mentioned in Hinduism. The other two are: Kriyamana Karma and Prarabda Karma. Sanchita Karma is the accumulated result of all your actions from all your past lifetimes. This is your total cosmic debt. Every moment of every day either you are adding to it or you are reducing this cosmic debt. Such actions done by you are not ripe to give fruits immediately or on the spot, but take some time to ripen. Such Karmas are kept in abeyance, waiting for the opportune time to become ripe, to give fruits in future. Till then they remain in balance and are accumulated. Until their fructification, these Sanchita Karmas cannot be neutralized.

Moksha is the liberation from Samsara, the cycle of death and rebirth.

~ ~ ~

15 – Who is Responsible?

Rehman, aged seventy-three, lived with his wife Ramla, sixty-eight, in a palatial double-storied house facing the Vembanad Lake at Kumarakam in Kerala, India. He was reclining in an armchair watching rafts, barges, canoes, cruisers and houseboats carrying cargos, passengers and tourists to and fro, longing to be among them, voyaging with vibrant dreams and hopes.

"I too was spirited and jovial like them. Yes, in the prime of my youth. Gone are those happy days. I have to abide the laws of nature. Pleasures and pains are part of life. A hill has a valley. A sunny day is followed by a dark night. But can I nurture the hope that this, my winter, will be followed by a spring? Might be in the next world, or in the next birth," Rehman's mind drifted philosophically back to his past.

Rehman retired as the headmaster of the government high school, two kilometres away from his house. Ramla had only a high school education and hence has remained a housewife. They had a son and two daughters. The daughters married two businessmen; one settled in Thiruvananthapuram and the other at Thodupuzha. Only occasionally did they visit their parents. Even the phone calls were rare. Anwar, Rehman and Ramla's son, worked as an electrician in Oman. Since he was not very studious, Anwar had to end his education with a polytechnic certificate. Being their only son, the parents wanted him to be always with them. Since Kerala is a State where the majority are educated and employment opportunities few, neither Anwar nor his parents could fulfil their wish. Anwar was compelled to seek employment abroad and thus he got placement as an electrician in a company run by an Arab in Oman. Though the work was very risky, it was highly rewarding.

Rehman' family had no landed property except the 4300 square foot lot, which Rehman had bought with his meagre salary several years back. He'd built a small house with a tiled roof on it.

His reputation as a school teacher was high. He was 100 percent committed to his profession. Never in his professional life had he caned or even pinched his pupils. He was always against corporal punishment, while his colleagues were cane masters. Rehman won the hearts of his pupils and their parents through sheer love and compassion. The return of love and respect from his former pupils and the villagers was his only asset, and that made him content and happy in his retired old life. In the evenings. he went to the community hall of the *panchayat* (village council) and became involved in the literacy programme of the government, educating the illiterate old people who had been forced to discontinue their education in their childhood.

Ramla was becoming weaker and weaker. The joints of her limbs were very painful. Treatments were done in several hospitals, and she was diagnosed with severe arthritis. She stayed awake several nights, unable to sleep. She had to do all the domestic work, since servants were unavailable. So, Rahman and Ramla decided that they should get their son married. Anwar was already twenty-four and Muslim boys were normally married in the early twenties. Though Anwar was unwilling at first, finally he yielded to his parents' pressure. With the money he had earned, a double-storeyed house had already been built. Proposals of marriage came from several rich families. A bridegroom employed abroad had high demand in the marriage field. Photographs of the proposed girls were sent to Anwar and he selected a beautiful girl from among the photos. The marriage was fixed.

After a wait of two months, Anwar got leave for the marriage—for just twenty-five days. The wedding ceremony and the feast were conducted with all pomp. The bride was beyond doubt very beautiful—a perfect match to Anwar. Only ten days were left for their honeymoon. Anwar and his wife, Aisha, went to Ootty, an enticing hill resort in Tamil Nadu, as a honeymoon trip. They stayed there for two days. Connubial bliss seemed heavenly until the day for Anwar's departure arrived. Naturally, it was heartrending for both Anwar and Aisha to part. Tears ran like brooks over her cheeks. Anwar's eyes also sank in tears. The fact that he would get leave only after two years multiplied their agony. Rehman and Ramla also grieved at their son's departure.

Aisha telephoned Anwar every day after his departure, and they talked for hours. Anwar hired a chauffeur for his car at home, for Aisha didn't know how to drive. Rahul, the chauffeur, was young and handsome. Aisha's grief and loneliness gradually disappeared. She went out in the car almost every day for shopping, to movies, to her own house as well as her friends' houses. Neither Ramla nor Rehman could tell her what to do. After all, she needed to obey only her husband—that was her policy. Anwar was compelled to marry in order to get help for his mother. Rahul accompanied Aisha throughout and entertained her with silly jokes. He went home to his house at dusk and returned each morning.

Was Aisha crossing the *lakshmana rekha* of a bride, or was Rahul tempting her like Ravana? Ramla raised the doubt first, and Rehman found some sense in it. How could they warn Aisha or Rahul? Suppose their relationship was only that of good friends? The doubts in the house spread to the neighbourhood, and people started to gossip. Once, when Ramla hinted at such gossip to Aisha, she exploded. She remarked that people were jealous of her, or they should never accuse a woman who suffers from the absence of her husband. In fact, she called her husband every day and talked with him for several minutes.

Rehman had no courage to raise any doubt to Aisha. Similarly, it was unfair to raise the question to Anwar, which would damn him to suspicion and dejection. Moreover, Anwar would accuse them of compelling him to marry, leading to this catastrophe. Aisha gradually stopped communication with Rehman and Ramla. She was young, healthy and full of passion. It was true that she was a bride, but her body knew no ethics. Who would satiate her carnal needs? How long could she control her desires? How could she resist the enticement? Was it fair for her husband to leave her hungry for such a long time? Could Anwar be blamed as he was against the marriage itself? Who was to be blamed, then?

Things were going like this with gloom and despair haunting Rehman's house. Ramla's health was deteriorating, and she staggered as she walked. Yet she did the cooking in the morning, since Aisha always got up late. One day, as usual, Ramla finished her cooking in the morning and was waiting for her husband and Aisha for the breakfast. As Aisha did not come down, Ramla went upstairs to her bedroom. The room was open, but she was not there. Ramla called her loudly, but there was no reply. It was evident that she had gone out of the house. Rehman searched for her in the neighbourhood in vain. He then went to Rahul's house and learned that he too was missing absent. Rehman came to the conclusion that Rahul had eloped with Aisha.

"My God, why do you test us like this? What sin have we committed? How will I report the matter to my son? How can we withstand this scandal? What will happen to Ramla when she finds out? What's the use in complaining to the police?" Such answerless questions crushed Rehman's mind as he walked back to his house.

"Could you find her? Is Rahul there in his house?" Ramla asked him as he stepped into the house.

"Rahul is missing, too," Rehman murmured.

"Allah, save our son! The whore has run after Saithan!" Saying this, she sank into her bed. With the assistance of the neighbours, she was taken to the hospital and admitted to the intensive care unit. The doctor reported that she was paralysed.

"Shouldn't we inform Anwar?" one of the neighbours asked Rehman.

"How can I inform my son that his wife has eloped with the chauffeur? What use is there in informing him that his mother is hospitalised because of it? He won't be able to get any leave and come back. When he calls me, I'll tell him," Rehman replied.

After a few days, Ramla was discharged and brought back to the house. Rehman's brother brought a maidservant named Shahana from his neighbourhood. She would serve the house from dawn to dusk and then return to her house.

Reminiscence of his past, sweet and then bitter, passed through Rehman's mind for nearly an hour. His heaven-like house had now declined to a hell of sorrow and dejection. Anwar has not called since Aisha's disappearance. Though Rehman tried to contact his son, there was no reply from the other end. What had happened to him? Had someone informed him about Aisha's departure? Rehman's worrying thoughts were interrupted by the appearance of the postman. Rehman had a registered letter. It was from the Sultanate of Oman. With shaking hands he opened the letter. The contents of the letter made him hysteric. The letter read that Anwar was dismissed from his company as he had been arrested by the government under the charge of involvement in terrorist activities.

Rehman yelled, "No, my son can never be a terrorist. I have taught him the noble values of secularism. He believes in the Creator, the only God who fosters the whole human race and preserves the universe. How can he work as a jihadist or for a faction who believes in genocide? God, why don't you call me back? I can't bear this. I want to die. I want to die." The maidservant rushed to him, hearing his loud cry.

"Sir, what happened to you?"

"I have lost my son, Shahana. Is your madam still sleeping?"

"Yes, Sir. Should I wake her?"

"Oh no. Please don't inform her. Anwar has lost his job. He is arrested for terrorism. Shahana, please don't tell this to others. Shahana, can you give me some poison? I don't want to live anymore."

"Sir, what are you saying? Nothing will happen to your son. He will be released. He can never be a terrorist, for he is your son. If you die, who is there for madam?"

"My God, why do you test me like this?" Saying this, he went to his room and shut the door. Shahana, as usual, went back to her house at 6 p.m. after her routine work. She hadn't told the lady what she had heard from the master. She prayed to God to give strength to his master to bear the misfortune.

Early the next morning, Shahana came to her master's house. The front door was still shut. She pressed on the doorbell. No one came to open the door. She pressed the bell again, but there was no reply. She called the master loudly, "Sir, please open the door. I am Shahana."

There was no response. She went round the house to the back door. It was open. She got into the kitchen and called for the master. Still there was no answer. Shahana rushed directly to the lady's bedroom where the husband and the wife slept at night. To her horror, she found the lady drenched in blood. She cried loudly, "God forbid! Madam, what happened to you?"

She turned to the cot where the master slept. He, too, was drenched in blood. She wailed, "How tragic! What villain has done this?"

Yelling loudly, she ran out of the house to call the neighbours. The neighbours rushed to the bedroom and found that Rehman and Ramla were stabbed to death. The beds became pools of stinky blood. The police came and searched every nook and cranny of the house for any evidence of the crime. They discovered that the safe where ornaments and money were kept was opened and the contents were stolen. The news of the merciless twin murder flashed around the village and the entire state like lightning. Thousands flooded to the house.

As mentioned earlier, the Rehman family was respectable and dear to the whole village. Police completed the formalities. The inquest and post-mortem continued for hours. The police dog searched for the murderer in vain. Rehman's daughters, their husbands and children sat round the dead bodies, crying and weeping. The whole house became a hell of wails. The dead bodies were buried in the afternoon. Several hundred mourners attended the function. The minister from the constituency assured the crowd that the murderer would be caught immediately. The police might catch the culprit, but there was statistically only a fifty percent chance. Who was to be blamed for the tragedy of Rehman and his family? When thousands of villainous wolves flourish and reign, innocent lambs like Rehman are mercilessly butchered. Where is poetic justice?

~ ~ ~

16 – Matthews, the Real Christian

This is the story of Matthews, aged fifty. He lived with his wife and two children in the State of Kerala in India. Though he had a Doctorate in Political Science, he was unemployed. While qualified for the post of lecturer, he has not had the luck of teaching students. He was one among the thousands of highly qualified candidates shut out from employment opportunities. Unemployment is the worst curse of Kerala, where literacy is ninety-five percent, and nearly twenty percent of the population are graduates. Matthews had faced many interviews and done exceptionally well. Since most of the schools and colleges are in the private sector, what they want is not the best candidate but one who gives the maximum amount. Schools and colleges—particularly engineering and medical colleges—are the best investments and they come up as mushrooms. Unlike mushrooms, they thrive and multiply.

Matthews knocked door after door for any employment, and frustrated, he went back to agriculture on his inherited farm of two acres. He gave in to the demands of his parents, and got married at the age of thirty. His spouse, Mercy was an unemployed woman with a post-graduate degree. They had a son named George and a daughter named Daisy.

Matthews had been a socialist in ideology since his teenage years. Highly intelligent and rational, he couldn't compromise to the funda-mentalism of religions. Religions seemed to him as a cleric's means of livelihood through the exploitation of the laity. Though a socialist, he believed in the existence of God. Matthews never went to church or took part in prayer gatherings in houses. Mercy, a devout Catholic, attended Masses and rites in the church near their house. Once when the parish priest asked Matthews why he avoided church, his reply was this: "Father, I am an Indian and like a true Indian I believe that God is in me. *Aham Brahmasmi* (I am God). Why should I seek him elsewhere?" The priest had no reply and went back to the church, thinking that Matthews could not be deceived like any other layman.

Matthews worked on his farm until five in the evening. He enjoyed every moment of this labour. There were coco palms, nutmeg trees, cocoa trees, banana plants, coffee plants and so on. He cleared weeds, fertilised, watered and collected fruits. He took a radio to the farm and played music for the plants' growth. To the accompaniment of music, his hands moved and the trees and plants danced to the tune with the gentle movement of their leaves and branches.

He raised cows, goats, chickens, ducks, cats and dogs, which gave him and his family untold happiness. After his work on the farm, he took a bath and went to the *panchayat* (village governing body) library and spent two hours with books and periodicals. Then he visited the recreation club where nearly twenty friends—old and young—waited for his discussion on various topics. He taught them what he had read from the books.

Matthews was a man of principles, a pure vegetarian, and a follower of Gandhi and Nehru. He shared his philosophy of life with them. He spoke to them about the relationship between Man, Nature and God; how man is related to other beings; how sinful it is to kill and eat animals, birds and fish; about democracy, socialism and dictatorship; corruption of politicians and clergy; the necessity of fighting against corruption, superstitions and all other evils in society. The people of the village took him as their guru or teacher.

Matthews sent his children to government schools. George was studying for an undergraduate degree in a government college in town and Daisy was at the tenth standard in a nearby government school. Though the standard of education in the government schools and colleges was poor, Matthews wasn't willing to sacrifice his principles by giving high donations and fees to private schools and colleges.

Election to the panchayat came and both the political fronts of the State—the Right Wing and the Left Wing started hunting for sure-win candidates. The Left Wing local leaders, knowing well the leftist ideology of Matthews, approached him and requested to stand as their candidate.

He told them: "Though I am socialist in my ideology, I don't want to be labelled as your man. I like and admire the teaching of Marx, Engel and Lenin. But do you follow what they have taught you? Many of your State level leaders are millionaires and corrupt. How can they represent the poor? So I can't stand as your candidate."

The local leaders were not willing to leave him and they pressured him to stand as an independent candidate supported by the Left Wing. As pressures came from his close friends as well, he gave the assent. He vowed that he would not spend any money for the campaign. The Left

Wing was willing to meet the expense. The nomination papers were filed. He visited house after house, accompanied by his friends and party men.

His chief opponent, the Right Wing candidate, was also another Catholic, but he did not have any public opinion. Needless to say, Matthews had a thumping victory. Thus Matthews' radiance started to spread from his village to the total panchayat. The Left Wing won a majority in the panachayat council and Matthews was elected the president of the panchayat. As President, he was very efficient, amicable and diplomatic, and hence won love and respect of the opposition members as well.

Because schools came under the jurisdiction of the panchayat, Matthews was invited to every official function in the schools. As stated earlier, in Kerala, government schools and colleges are very few compared to government-aided schools and colleges run by private agencies. The Government gives a salary to the teachers and maintenance grants to the management, but the appointment authority rests in the hands of the private management.

The Christians who run the majority of schools and colleges are a minority here like the Muslims, and they enjoy the minority right to appoint anyone they like, getting hundreds of thousands of rupees as donations. The Indian Constitution and the Supreme Court give them the provision to do this practice. In such an aided school, Matthews was invited to preside over the School Day celebrations. In his presidential address, he touched many ethical issues related to the school.

He spoke: "Dear teachers, you should be honest in your words and actions. Our aided and government schools face great challenge and threats from unaided English medium[6] schools. These unaided schools hook parents to send their children there, paying high donations and fees. Consequently, there are losses of class-division in our schools and you teachers are either transferred or remain protected staff. Aren't you also

---

[6] *Medium* is used in the sense of which medium of language is used for education. In Kerala, as well as other States of India, the first language or mother tongue is not English. English is only the second language. In all the States of India, there are two kinds of medium of instruction in schools. Government schools in the majority of the cases are mother-tongue medium schools where all the subjects like pure science, mathematics, arts and other social sciences are taught in the mother-tongue of the State. English is taught there only as a second language. In most of the private schools, the medium of instruction of these same subjects is in English.

responsible for the problem? How many of your children are studying in our schools?" Shamefaced, the teachers bent their heads, afraid to face him anymore.

On another occasion, at a seminar on the topic "Secularism in India," conducted by the panchayat council itself, where leaders of different religions were seated on the stage, Matthews exploded: "I request our religious leaders not to mix religion with politics. Let religion go its way and politics its way. Hasn't Christ taught us, 'Give unto Caesar, Caesar's and unto God, God's?' You should not request laymen to vote for this party or that man. Your rights will be safeguarded by courts if politicians or governments encroach them...

"It is high time we stop discrimination against women. Being the children of God, there is no difference between man and woman. Then why should they be denied entry in God's abode? Do you think Ayyappa Swamy (Lord Shiva's son) will be angry if women get into his temple at Sabarimala? Do you think Allah will be embittered if women get into mosques to pray to Him? Do you think if a woman celebrates Mass in a church your God will be angry or the altar defiled? These are all remnants of patriarchy and sheer injustice to women." You can imagine the reaction of the religious leaders on the stage. All of them quit, the place murmuring abuse at Matthews.

Matthews continued his mission of opening the eyes of the people. As the President, he did whatever possible for the welfare of the people. He was successful in getting more and more funds from the State and Central governments for developments in the panchayat. Though clergy and religious leaders were against him, laymen gave him full support. The religious leaders realized the threat, and setting apart their differences of ideology, they unanimously took a decision to pluck the hold of Matthews on their people.

Election to the State Assembly came, and the Left Wing approached Matthews again for the contest. Matthews was well aware that the religious leaders were against him and they would dissuade their people from electing him. So he said no to the party men who approached him. Then the Chief Minister himself visited him and compelled him to stand as an independent candidate supported by the Left Wing. He reminded Matthews that good representatives like him were needed by the people and the State. Matthews yielded to the CM's request and nomination papers were filed.

The Right Wing candidate was also a Catholic, Mr. John, a multi-millionaire distiller. Mr. John was given full support by the religious leaders of the three major religions—Christianity, Islam and Hindu. They gave several lakhs to his election fund. In the campaign—notices, posters, banners, flex boards, mic announcements—the Right Wing candidate was several miles ahead of Matthews. Still the survey in the newspapers showed that Matthews would come out victorious.

It alarmed the Right Wing camp, especially the religious leaders. They published and read pastoral letters in churches and sent emissaries to each house, pleading for a vote for the Right Wing candidate. There were hundreds of people to campaign for Matthews. He was accompanied by nearly fifty men, women and children bearing placards of his photograph when he visited the houses. None had any doubt that Matthews would have an overwhelming majority of one lakh votes over the Right Wing candidate.

The day of the election came and there was heavy polling in the constituency. Ninety percent of the voters went to the polling booths. The Left Wing camp was very happy and there was no doubt about Matthews' victory. On the contrary, the Right Wing camp was gloomy and they were sure that their candidate would fail. The results would come only after six days.

The day after the election, as usual, Matthews got up early in the morning and went for a forty-five minutes' walk along the deserted street. He was very cautious to walk along the right side of the street. A vehicle came from behind and struck him. He fell unconscious on the street with a bleeding head. The vehicle disappeared without stopping there. There were no witnesses. Some pedestrians who came along the street took him to the government hospital.

The doctor did nothing as Matthews was dead on arrival. The news flashed in the village and spread the whole State. Different news channels of TV announced the tragic death of Matthews to the whole world through 'flash news.' The hospital was crowded by people. Matthews' wife, Mercy fainted when she heard the news.

After a post-mortem, the body was brought back to the house. The children started crying and sobbing, sitting at the coffin. The whole house echoed with wails and sobs. Mercy, who had recovered from her torpor, put her head on Matthews' cheek, crying and sobbing. Ministers and State level political leaders came and paid homage to the dead hero.

Burial was fixed for five in the evening. Matthews' brother, Joseph visited the parish priest and sought permission for the burial in the cemetery. Without any compassion, the priest replied: "How can Matthews be buried in the cemetery? He is not a Christian. He does not attend Mass, make confessions or receive Eucharist. Hence his name is not in the parish register."

"Father, it's true that he didn't go to church. But wasn't he baptized? He was a true Christian in spirit and led a life as Christ has shown to his people. Moreover we do have a family tomb in the cemetery for which we have paid the amount you have requested. So we have the right to bury his body here."

"Mr. Joseph, there is no need of any argument between us. The canon rule doesn't allow us to bury him here. I shall report the case to the bishop and if he permits, the body can be buried."

"OK, Father, you may decide whatever you like, but we will bring the body here for the burial. Will you come to our house for the burial rites?"

"Not likely."

"Right. Father, I am leaving."

Joseph came back to the house and reported the matter to the closest relatives and friends assembled there. They decided that at any cost the body would be buried in the family tomb.

At 5 pm, the burial rites started. As the priest was absent, one pious elder read the prayer for the dead accompanied by dirges from the crowd. The body was taken to the church in an ambulance. Hundreds followed it on foot in long procession. The front door of the church was shut and the parish priest stood on the veranda along with the sexton and the cook.

"Father, please open the door and let the body get into the church," Matthews' brother Joseph cried.

"No, I haven't got the permission from the bishop."

"Then allow us to bury the body in our tomb. Please open the gate of the cemetery."

"No, the bishop hasn't allowed."

"Brother, please listen to what I say," Matthews' wife, Mercy exploded in a choking sound. "We will leave the body here on the veranda. Let them do what they like. Father, my husband is far more a Christian than you people. Please don't forget that you are only one among us, only our representative, and not the representative of God as you falsely claim. My dear relatives and friends, let's go back. Let them do what they like with my husband's body."

The whole crowd assembled there started to retreat. Suddenly, the sexton was sent by the priest to Mercy who had gone a few steps from the church. The sexton told her that the priest was willing to bury the body.

"Let the Father announce it and apologise to the crowd for dishonouring my dead husband," she replied. The priest did so, and the gate of the cemetery was opened and the body was buried in the family tomb without any prayers by the priest. No prayers were needed from the priest, not even from Matthews' wife, since angels had already borne his soul to heaven.

The result of the election came out after five days. Matthews won the seat by a margin of 150,000 votes over the Right Wing candidate. There couldn't be any celebration by the Left Wing. The Right Wing won the majority of seats in the State. There was no wonder in it because religions played a major role behind the victory.

Matthews' assassins could not be found. The police are still searching for the murderers. How far will it be successful is to be found in the wake of the shifting of power. Let's hope that Matthews' death will be avenged by the court of law.

~ ~ ~

17 – Multicultural Harmony

Amar, Akbar and Anthony are good neighbours living with their families in the village called Devalokam in Kottayam District of the Indian State Kerala (popularly known as "God's own country"). As the name suggests, Devalokam is indeed heavenly—both the topography and the people give it a celestial touch. Rubber plantations, coconut trees, rice paddy fields, and small brooks flowing like snakes make the village ever green and enticing. It seems that gods from above descend through the tall coconut trees and communicate with humans and other beings. Hindus and Christians are the major communities and Muslims are a minority there. They all have lived in perfect harmony and symbiosis. There are temples, churches and mosques chanting peoples' gratitude to God for showering all these blessings.

Amar is a farmer living with his wife Seetha, son Anand and daughter Aswathy. He has five acres of agricultural land with a rubber plantation, rice paddy field, coconut trees, and so on. Amar and Seetha have only high school education and they passed tenth class. When the story begins, their son, Anand, is studying in the tenth class and daughter, Aswathy, is in the seventh class.

Akbar is a business man, a timber merchant. Though he doesn't possess much landed property, he earns well through his business. He lives happily with his wife, Ramla, daughter, Laila, and son, Wahab. Akbar and Ramla too have only a high school education, the former having completed ninth class and the latter tenth class. Laila is studying in the same tenth class as Anand, and Wahab is in the eighth class.

Anthony is an upper-division clerk in the Department of Education at Kottayam. He has passed the Pre-Degree Course. He lives with his wife, Alphonsa, a housewife who passed the tenth class. They have a daughter, Celine studying in the same tenth class as Anand and Laila. Their son, Joseph is studying in the seventh class with Aswathy. All these neighbouring children attend the Government High School, Devalokam.

Amar, Akbar, Anthony had their school education together in the same Government School, the same class till the ninth, when Akbar failed and the others passed over to the tenth. They never had a feeling that they belonged to different religions. Their parents brought them up in such a secular manner that religion never mattered in their social life. Religious festivals of Onam, Vishu, Christmas, Easter, Ramzan, Bakrid were common festivals and they celebrated them, inviting others and their families to their houses and feasting together.

Once when there were returning from the school after the classes, Antony said: "Haven't you noted what our biology master taught today? He was teaching us the evolution theory. The theory proves that man has been evolved from ape-like ancestors. But our Bible teaches us that the first man Adam was moulded by God out of earth and breathed life to it. And the first woman Eve was created out of Adam's rib. And that the entire universe was created for them."

Akbar replied: "True, we are also taught the same thing in the book of Genesis."

Then Amar said: "Unlike your religions' teachings, which you study through Sunday school and Madrasa, we Hindus are not taught anything religious. We read our scriptures and our parents impart us great lessons of our religion. We believe in *Paramatma* and *jivatma*, universal soul and individual soul, and thus all other beings are siblings of human beings. The element of God is among all creations, living and non-living. In my opinion we should believe and follow what science has taught us, because it is proved beyond any doubt. Similarities between apes and humans are many and why can't we believe that man is evolved from apes?"

Akbar and Anthony agreed with Amar's views. Akbar added: "When evolution is taken from the religious point of view, God the Father is the creator of the universe and all creations are His children. So naturally we human beings are siblings of other beings on earth. If the relationship between God and man is thus a father-son relation, why should there be innumerable religions and gods among us?"

Anthony replied: "What you have stated is hundred percent true, dear friend. In fact, religions were created out of selfishness of man—thirst for power and wealth. Now the religions have degenerated to such a state that their primary motive is exploitation of the ignorant, illiterate, superstitious masses."

Amar: "Well stated, dear friends. When we know that God the Father is the creator of this entire universe, why should we need any religion to love and honour our Father? God has given us the divinity and reasoning power to understand what is right and what is wrong. Besides, we have governments and civil codes in our country and we know we have to abide by the laws of nature."

Meanwhile they reached the gates of their houses and thus ended the healthy discussion.

~ ~ ~

Years passed smoothly, and the friendship and harmony among the three families strengthened. They never felt that they belonged to different religions, but lived as members of one joint family. Amar's son, Anand, completed his engineering degree and got an appointment with the Wipro Company at Bangalore. Anthony's daughter, Celine, also studied in the same engineering college with Anand, completed her bachelor's of Technology and got a job in the same Wipro Company at Bangalore.

They were in love with each other from the school level itself but kept it top secret, fearing that the parents might object to their inter-religious marriage. They knew very well that even if the parents consented to their marriage, the society and the religious leaders would object to it because the Kerala society has become so religiously fanatic. But love knows no religion, and they continued to love like two pigeons, unnoticed by others. They resolved to marry after a few years even if the parents objected to it.

Once a month, they came home, taking a one day leave from the office. Sundays are holidays and so they got two full days to spend there. Their travelled by night bus. One Sunday, when Celine was at home, her father, Anthony, called her to his room. Her mother, Alphonsa, was also there.

Anthony said, "Celine, you are now 25 and we have to think of your marriage. The neighbours as well as our relatives are asking when that will be."

Celine replied: "Father, why should we be in a hurry? Let's wait for two more years."

Then Alphonsa interfered, "Why should we wait? It's already late now. We have no liabilities. Then why should we wait?"

Anthony said: "Daughter, why do you object to a marriage now? Are you waiting for someone? I mean, do you have somebody in your mind? Tell me frankly."

Celine mustered all courage and replied: "Yes father, I am in love with a person."

Alphonsa asked: "Who is that man?"

Celine said: "I am in love with Anand and we have decided to marry."

Celine and Anthony were shocked to hear this. Both of them burst out, "No, we won't allow you to marry him."

Celine was determined. "What's wrong with Anand? Isn't he a good natured man? You all love him as your own son, don't you? Isn't he handsome enough and healthy? Hasn't he good income for livelihood? Isn't their family respectable? Aren't his parents your close friends? Then why do you object?"

Anthony said: "Daughter, all you say Anand and his parents are true. But they belong to another religion. Do you think our relatives as well as the parish priest will agree to this marriage? If it happens, we will be treated as dissidents, do you know? How can we live here disobeying our religion?

Celine replied: "True, we are aware of it and we have decided to live in Bangalore after the marriage. There, no religion will persecute us. It is such a secular society. Anand says that if his parents object to the marriage as per Hindu rites, we will have it conducted and registered officially in the Registrar's office."

Anthony said: "As long as I live, I won't allow it."

Having said this, he visited Amar next door. There he called, "Amar, please come out. Call your son also."

"Good morning Anthony. What's the matter?"

"Ask your son, Anand. What harm have we done to you and your family? Your son is trying to defame us and outlaw us from our religion. We have been living as brothers and how could your son think of defaming us by planning to marry my daughter? You should have dissuaded your son from such a connection. Instead you promoted it. We will never allow it.

Amar replied "Anthony, mind your words. Do you think we would encourage our son into such an inter-religious marriage? Why couldn't you dissuade your daughter from loving him?"

"Your son might have bewitched her or she would not have fallen into his trap."

Amar was now equally furious. "Shut up your mouth and get out of my compound. It is your daughter who bewitched my son."

"I have come here not to stay but to warn you. Tell your son to drop his plan. Let him seek some other lady from his own religion. No more shall you and your family enter into our compound." Telling this, Anthony returned home.

Thus the bosom friends Amar and Anthony became foes to each other. The long friendship of more than forty-five years was broken by the arrow of religion. Religion which should unite the minds, here divided two families. Akbar tried to unite his friends Amar and Anthony and their families as a mediator. But since both the families were inflamed by religious sentiments, his words fell on deaf ears. Still, the secret love between Anand and Celine continued. There was great pressure from both the families and relatives to break their love and, abandon their decision to marry. The parish priest came to Anthony's house and warned the family of consequences if the marriage took place.

Needless to say, the accusations and threats from the family members, relatives, and the religious leaders affected Celine's peace of mind. Because of a continuous severe headache for days, she took leave from the firm and returned home. She was admitted in a hospital and was found that she had high blood pressure. Even after treatments of several days in the hospital, the blood pressure could not be controlled. It was diagnosed that the high blood pressure caused severe damage to her kidneys. Her health was becoming worse.

She was taken to a kidney specialist hospital in the city. She longed to see Anand, but he was afraid to visit her in the hospital as her parents did not welcome him. All he could do was to pray for her speedy recovery. Further diagnoses proved that both her kidneys were damaged to such an extent that only kidney transplantation could save her life. Anthony was not rich enough to afford the hundred thousand rupees needed to find a living donor.

The entire village of Devalokam knew of this tragedy. People prayed for her life. The neighbours, parish priest, pujari of the temple, imam of the mosque visited the hospital and shared their sorrows with Anthony's family. Since Celine was in the intensive care unit, they could have only a glimpse of her through the glass window.

Anand knew all developments through Akbar. He told him that he was willing to donate one of his kidneys to save his darling. Akbar conveyed Anand's intention to Anthony and the family. Since it was the last straw to save his daughter Anthony and Alphonsa agreed to the proposal. Then Akbar visited Amar's house and disclosed Anand's wish to the parents, Amar and Seetha. They were terribly shocked at Anand's wish. Then Amar called his son and asked: "Anand what nonsense are you speaking? You are very young and how can you live with one kidney? If it is affected by some disease, your life will be over."

Anand replied: "Dad, I don't want to have a future life without Celine. So, to save her life, I am prepared to do any sacrifice. Besides, there are many men who have donated one of their kidneys and lead very healthy lives. If we are careful in our lifestyle, we need not bother about our health. I have decided to donate my kidney if they are willing to accept it."

Amar said: "If that's your decision, let it happen. Saving one's life is a great satvik karma."

Akbar relayed the great decision to Anthony and Alphonsa, and they were immensely relieved and happy. The news flashed all over the village, and the people glorified Anand's sublime decision. Anand was called to the hospital and made all lab tests as to find out if his kidney can be accepted by Celine's body. Fortunately both Anand and Celine had ABO blood group and it cross matched.

All the formalities of kidney donation were completed soon, and Anand's kidney was successfully transplanted into Celine's body after several hours of surgery. Greatly relieved and overwhelmed with joy, both Amar and Anthony embraced each other, shedding tears and asking for forgiveness. Similarly, Seetha and Alphonsa hugged each other and shed tears of joy. Akbar and his family too shared in this happiness and the reunion of the two families.

Hundreds of the villagers including the parish priest, pujari, and imam were waiting outside the hospital for the result. They all celebrated the successful transplantation. Amar, Anthony, and their families along with Akbar and his family came out of the operation theatre block. They requested the pujari, parish priest and imam to come near to them. Then Anthony said, "Respected Purjari, Reverend Father, respected Imam and our loving countrymen, This is to inform you that my daughter's life was saved by the sacrifice of Anand. So Amar and myself and our families have decided to conduct the marriage of Celine and Anand. We will conduct it after three months on an auspicious day and the marriage will take place as per Hindu rites."

Amar then said, "We solicit honourable Pujari, Father and Imam to be present for the ceremony and bless our children."

The Pujari said: "We are only happy to be part of this purest union of two souls."

The parish priest added: "It is God Almighty who has united them, sharing their organs, and our religions shall take it in that sense, giving full support to God's plans. We will surely be present for the function and will bless the ideal couple."

The Imam said: "This is God's plan and man shall not try to make any obstructions. I will be present for the function to bless the noble couple."

Thus Anand married Celine at Maha Vishnu Temple on 9th November. The pujari led the rites and the parish priest and imam were beside him, showering blessings on the couple. All the villagers were present. After the wedding, there was the vegetarian dinner, at which all feasted with great happiness.

It became a golden day for the largest multicultural country in the world. It added beauty to the wonderful enticing face of India—unity in diversity. Another mellifluous string was added to the multicultural symphony and harmony of India. Witnessing it, the entire world smiled.

~ ~ ~

18 – A Good Samaritan

I am going to narrate an incident that is three-quarters real, and the rest blended with fantasy to make it a short story. The event took place in a town in Kerala, India.

In order to attend a seminar at Thrissur, I was driving my car along the national highway. Cars, buses and trucks were running like rockets along the black ribbon of the roadway. Dusk was approaching and the light of the vehicles went past like missiles. Suddenly I noticed a man-like object on the left side of the road. I steered my car to the side and applied the brake. There was a man lying unconscious, and bleeding through his nostrils. I felt his pulse and understood that life had not yet departed from him. He was a lean man, aged around sixty, and I lifted him into my car using all my strength. I drove the car quickly to the nearest hospital, some five kilometres away at Thrissur. A vehicle had hit him and thrown him to the side of the road.

The driver of the vehicle sped away, fearing the consequences. Such iron-hearted people are characteristic of selfish, cutthroat, contemporary urban society. The accident victim was admitted to Amala Hospital, Thrissur. The nurses rushed in and I told them how he had been found and picked up. After an examination, the doctor reported to me that the patient was critical. He had a severe head injury. An immediate operation was required and I told him to do whatever was needed to save his life. I signed the papers for the patient as none of his relatives was present. I advanced an amount of Rs. 10,000 from my purse as the fees of the operation. Before the patient was shifted to the operating theatre, I asked the doctor if he had discovered the man's identity. The doctor produced a wallet that had been found in his pocket. The victim's identity card was there in the wallet along with a phone diary.

From the identity card, I knew that he was Mr. Xavier, residing at Chavakad, a place not very far from Thrissur. The phone book helped me to call to his house.

"Hello, is this Mr. Xavier's house?" I asked through my cell phone.

"Yes, kindly tell me who you are," replied a female voice.

"I am Professor Mohan. You may not know me. Are you Xavier's wife?"

"Yes, what's the matter?"

"He has met with an accident and is admitted at Amala Hospital, Thrissur. Don't worry. Not very serious. Please come to the hospital."

"Jesus, save my husband! I am coming soon," came out her choking sound.

Within half an hour, Xavier's wife, Mariam, arrived there, accompanied by a dozen other people. She couldn't control herself and was crying aloud, tears running like streams. At her request, I told her what had happened. She cried aloud to Jesus to save her husband. The corridor before the operation theatre echoed with the wails of Mariam, her two daughters, and Xavier's parents. I tried my best to pacify them. A few hours passed. More and more people flooded to the passage. There were some twenty-five people—men and women—assembled there praying for his life.

I started to wonder how such an ordinary-seeming person could inspire so many people to despair for him, and pray for his life. The sobs and wails shook the walls of the corridor and the nurses couldn't control the situation. Fortunately, a nurse opened the door of the operating theatre and asked me to meet the doctor inside. I longed for good news from the doctor and prayed to God to save Xavier. The doctor told me that the operation was successful. Xavier has survived the crucial condition, but it was uncertain as to whether he could lead a normal life. The brain was affected, and he could possibly suffer paralysis, as well as loss of memory.

If this news was imparted to Xavier's kith and kin waiting outside, I could imagine the hellish wail erupting there. Mariam would collapse, and have to be admitted to the hospital herself. Hence, I pleaded the doctor to tell them a lie and thus hide the seriousness of the case. Accordingly, the doctor appeared before them and announced that Xavier had had only a minor head injury and there had been a blood clot inside, which was successfully removed. He could be expected to recover soon, and would be discharged within a week. The people, including Mariam, were relieved and the wailing ceased.

My eagerness to know why so many people were anxious about Xavier's health sprouted in my mind and I couldn't but seek the answer. I preferred to stay there a little longer. After all, I had nothing more to do that night than sleeping in a lodge at Thrissur to attend the seminar the following day.

"Mariam, kindly tell me where you are from and who are all these people?"

"Sir, we are much obliged to you for saving my husband's life. You are an angel whom Jesus sent," she replied in a broken voice. I prayed to God to give them the strength to bear. *Oh my God, they are relieved by the lie from the doctor. Once they come to know the reality, how will they face it?*

"We live at Chavakad, my husband Xavier, these two daughters, and these parents. The daughters Liz and Grace are studying in the eighth standard[7]."

"What's your occupation?"

"We have two acres of agricultural land and we live on it."

"And who are these people?"

The answers came from several quarters at once.

"I am Venugopal. I met with a road accident five years ago. Had not this Xavier *chettan*[8] (elder brother) taken me to the hospital, then I would be in the next world now."

"The same is the case with me also. My name is Akbar. While I was going on my bike, a truck crashed into me from behind and threw me away. Like an angel, Xavier chettan appeared and took me to the hospital. I owe my life to him."

"I am Joseph. Three years back, while I was pushing my vegetable cart along the highway, a truck smashed into me and my cart, and I fell unconscious. When I opened my eyes, I was in the hospital, picked up and saved by this great man Xavier. He is indeed a saviour as his name designates."

"Sir," Mariam continued the conversation for others. "What you hear from them is true. These are only a few of the men my husband has saved from the accidents. My husband has saved five hundred and ten people from the road accidents in the past eight years. We have taken it as our mission to save the lives of men who are uncared for on roadsides. My

---

[7] First standard, second standard, and so on are the equivalent of first grade, second grade, and so forth in the USA.

[8] *Chettan* is the term used in India for calling one's elder brother. The same term is used for calling any man senior by age to a person. Its feminine term is 'chechi'. In India, people don't address anyone older by name. If such person is a government official or a venerable person, they address him/her as sir/madam. Similarly all respectable persons irrespective of their age are addressed by sir/madam.

daughters and I help my husband in nursing the accident victims in the hospital. There were several cases in which the relatives of the victims never turned up and we had pay the hospital charges ourselves. Forty-nine victims have died on my husband's lap on his way to the hospital. How uneasy was my husband in those days! He couldn't eat anything and I had to wipe the tears which ran through his cheeks." Mariam's eyes were immersed in tears and she mopped it with a kerchief.

"Don't cry, Mariam. God will reward you," I tried to console her.

"Yes sir, how can Jesus reject us? What have we done that He punishes my husband like this?" she started sobbing.

"God will never punish you, Mariam. He only loves His creations and never punishes."

"Yes sir, I too believe so. My husband had earlier been an employee of a private bus company. He had seen so many such accidents then where victims had been uncared for. Then, 20th February 2000, when I was walking along the road with my only son, William, an auto rickshaw hit my son from behind. He was taken immediately to the hospital but he left us forever after eight days. He was only twelve then." She couldn't stop crying. Mariam continued her sobs for a few minutes and then resumed her narration.

"That tragic end of our son inspired my husband to involve himself in such humanitarian service. Every day from 10:30 am to 2 pm, my husband has been at Guruvayoor, ready to rescue such accident victims. From 2:30 pm to 6 pm was be available at Kunnamkulam. Very often, my husband had to spend the money in his pocket for such hospital service and we often starved as a result. By the grace of God, we are being helped in this service by my husband's brother in the Gulf as well as from my own parents."

"God has many more plans to complete through your husband, Mariam. So Xavier will recover soon. He is indeed that good Samaritan of your Bible."

"Yes sir, God will save him, we're sure." The words came out from the mouths of all the people assembled there and it echoed from corridor to corridor. No doubt God will do a miracle here, my mind murmured.

~ ~ ~

19 – An Email from Senthil Kumar

From   senthilkumar1975@yahoo.co.in
To   kvdominic@gmail.com
Hi Prof. Dominic,

I am really sorry for delaying my reply. When I opened my inbox, I found three of your mails expressing anguish and even anger, at my silence. I am sure when you read this mail your anger will dissolve and turn into sympathy.

As you know, my mother has been staying with me for several years and has been under treatment for a heart problem since 1990. When my wife and I go to the office, my mother is alone in the house as the housekeeper. Even though she is now eighty, she can still manage her personal affairs by herself. She used to take her food and medicine at regular times. So, things were going on very smoothly even in our absence from 9.30 am to 5.30 pm. Though I wanted to hire a servant, my wife was against it, since an outsider in our house would steal away our privacy. And my mother also insisted that she would manage herself without a servant or home-nurse.

My mother is over-sentimental by nature, and as she was aging this sentimentalism increased. The tragic or premature deaths of people as it appeared in the newspaper every day would move her mind to such an extent that she would start crying, tears flowing down her cheeks. Her doctor has advised us that her heart couldn't bear any tension or sorrow, and we should see that she was always happy. So we stopped subscription of the Tamil newspaper and managed with only *The Hindu*. My brothers, sisters and I came to a decision that no one would tell mother sad and unpleasant things whenever they visit her.

Meanwhile we were informed that my mother's younger sister, living with a family some fifty kilometres from our place, was admitted to hospital. She fell from her bed while getting up, and after that was unable to stand up or walk. We went to the hospital, telling mother that we were going for a marriage feast. We were sure that God would forgive us for this lie. When we reached the hospital we found that our aunt was in the

ICU and the doctor reported that she had had a stroke and had become paralysed.

We returned to our house in the evening. Mother enquired about the marriage dinner, the whereabouts of the spouse etc. etc. We had to add lies to lies to satisfy her. The aunt was discharged from the hospital after two weeks as the doctors could do nothing more. She is still bedridden and has now spent two years in bed—can't speak, can't remember, and must be spoon-fed. Of course, our mother lives here, quite ignorant of her sister's tragedy. She would sometimes enquire us about the aunt's news and request us to phone her. We would tell her that the aunt was perfectly healthy in her house. We have informed our cousins that we had told such an inevitable lie to our mother, and whenever they visit her they should not tell her the truth.

Once when one of my brothers met with an accident and broke his leg, I was compelled to tell mother that he had a little injury caused by some very minor bike accident. Suddenly mother started sobbing and the pumping of her heart slowed down. As the breathing became very slow and difficult, she was immediately admitted to hospital. After injections of medicine and supplemental oxygen, she recovered after one week. The doctor warned us against telling such sad news to her. Thank God, she has had a very poor memory since then, so that after she was discharged from the hospital she forgot about my brother's accident and his injury. She often asked me about that brother and why he was not visiting her. I would reply that he was very busy with his clothing business there in his town. After his recovery, he visited her as usual and she was happy at seeing him.

Then one day we received a phone call from the house of our uncle— mother's youngest brother, living some sixty kilometres away from our house—telling us that the uncle was admitted to hospital, and it was very serious. Telling mother another lie, we rushed to the hospital. The uncle was very critical and sinking fast. The doctor said that recovery was impossible. Uncle's lungs had severe sores and he would meet his end within a few days.

We were again in a dilemma. This uncle was our mother's favourite sibling. Since our mother's father and mother died young, it was our mother who had looked after him. She was indeed a mother to him. Whenever this uncle came to our house, the exchange of love between them often made us envious. Now, he was at his point of death, what shall we do? He wasn't not old, but only 65. What would happen to our mother if the news was imparted to her? We decided not to inform our mother of the uncle's critical case. But our prayer for his life was of no use and he died in the hospital after a week. We were telephoned about his death.

We were in a dilemma again. How could we tell our mother that her most beloved brother was no more? The very news was sure to end her life. Is it a sin to hide such fatal news from our mother? What would our relatives and other people say when they knew that we had hidden the news from her and not allowed her to see her dearest brother's still body before it was cremated? The doctor's warning echoed in our ears as mother's death knells. We thought about it over and again for several minutes. Finally we came to a conclusion that our mother's life was precious to us, and so we had to sustain her life. We went for the burial, telling mother another lie of attending a marriage. We announced to the bereaved family that mother was not in a position to travel so far.

Thus mother continued her life with only happy memories. In fact, her life was sustained by the heavy dose of medicines thrice a day. Another year passed slowly. One day as I was busy with files in my office, I received a phone call.

"Brother Senthil, it's me, Muthu, calling from your house. Please come fast, for mother's condition is very serious."

"Muthu, I am coming." I dashed to my house in my car. Mother was lying on her bed with her eyes shut and breathing with much difficulty. I cried, "Mother, mother." But she did not reply.

"Muthu, when did you come here?" I asked.

"I came fifteen minutes ago to invite you all to commemorate the anniversary of my father's death." Muthu is the eldest son of my above-mentioned uncle who passed away one year back.

"Oh, you then told mother the purpose of your visit. We hadn't informed mother of your father's death as it will worsen her condition," I explained.

"I didn't know that, brother. Very sorry," he apologized.

"Let's take mother to the hospital," I suggested. We did so immediately. The doctor gave her injections and oxygen. Her blood was drawn for diagnosis. I phoned to my wife, brothers and sisters. They all arrived at the hospital within half an hour. Mother was taken to the ICU and we were not permitted to see her. After two hours the doctor informed us that mother had had a severe stroke. The recovery seems impossible. Her life may drag on, but she is paralysed. Just like her younger sister, she too became bedridden. Mother was discharged from the hospital yesterday and lies in my house, longing for her death.

Hope you have understood my position. You can do nothing to soothe me. Kindly pray for my mother.

Love,
Senthil Kumar.

~ ~ ~

20 – Selvan's House

"Sir, sir," I heard someone calling me, so I opened the front door. There was Selvan, shedding tears. He wore a neat white *dhoti* and a light-coloured shirt.

"What happened, Selvan? Why are you crying," I enquired.

"The Engineer sir scolded me and sent me out of the house," Selvan was sobbing.

"When? At the blessing ceremony?"

"When the Reverend Father got into the house along with others for the blessing of the house, I too entered the room. Then the Engineer sir came near me and asked why I was there. He then asked me to leave the place. How can I bear it, sir? Haven't I been living in the house, guarding it for the past one and a half years from the very day the foundation stone was laid? How could he send me out, sir? There is not an inch of the building where I have not watered the mortar or plaster. I have been working hard wetting the structure—the roofs, the walls, the floors, the pillars, the compound walls, and so on. I have been serving him from dawn to late evening all these months. I have been the keeper of the house, sweeping the rooms, cooking my food, eating in the dining room, sleeping in one of the bedrooms till yesterday. Am I just a cat or a dog to shut me out? Haven't I the right to attend the blessing of the house, sir?"

I tried my best to console him. "Selvan, this is the way of the world. The masons, the carpenters, the plumbers, the electricians, painters and scores of labourers—who were the real builders of that house—were they invited for the blessing ceremony? No. You are also one of them. You are only the watchman, not the real owner of the house, aren't you? Take it that way. Don't be upset."

"True, sir. I am not the owner of the house and I am not going to live there for the rest of my life. Though that house is not mine, I have been looking after it as my own. But now I am out it. It's unbearable, sir. You can't feel my agony."

I was well aware that I could not console Selvan with my logic and philosophy. I just remembered the very first day he arrived here. He is a native of Kumily, the borderland to Tamil Nadu State. Though a Tamil man, he speaks a mix of Tamil and Malayalam. Selvan is a Christian, aged fifty-eight. His wife, Chellammaand children live in their house at Kumily. His eldest son is employed in Saudi Arabia. In fact, there had been no need for Selvan to come over here and keep security of this house under construction. His wife and children disliked his staying here alone for a meagre salary. But Selvan, being healthy enough, didn't like to stay idle in his house. He has only 1/10th of an acre of land, and there was no way to work it. Hence like Ulysses, he set out seeking independence and freedom.

Selvan always appeared as lively as a squirrel. My neighbour, Thomas, the Engineer, employed him as a security guard for the building materials. He was given only a low salary of Rs. 2500 per month. When Thomas found that Selvan was honest, innocent and meek, he tried to exploit him. He was made to work—watering the mortar and plaster, cleaning the premises, spading and removing the grass from the half-acre of land around the building and helping Thomas in his household a kilometre away.

Thus Selvan had to work from dawn to late evening. He cooked his rice and the curry was brought from Thomas's residence. He used to take his breakfast and lunch late after the wetting work. As the building progressed, Selvan's quantity of labour also increased. He demanded an increase in salary from Thomas, who raised his salary to Rs. 3000 but stopped the supply of curry. Poor Selvan consumed his rice with no curry, or with curry supplied to him from my house or by a neighbour, Mr. Thankappan. The only enjoyment he had was the intake of cheap liquor in the evening with two companions.

Selvan was a very talkative man. He appeared to be the overseer of the whole construction going on at the work site. He gave directions to masons and carpenters. His Tamil-toned banter always echoed within the premises. I have observed him giving advice even to the owner, Thomas. The labourers found in him a real friend and entertainer. His loud utterances amused me when I was sitting leisurely on the balcony. When any one—neighbours or strangers—came to have a look at the house, Selvan proudly led them inside and showed every nook and cranny, explaining what they were. He acted as the owner of the house.

Selvan wished to plant bananas on the barren land adjacent to the house, and Thomas gave him money for it. He planted nearly twenty bananas, and watered them every day during the summer. Once, when a labourer cut a leaf of a banana plant to use as a plate, Selvan warned him not to repeat it as it would slow down its growth. All the plants yielded rich fruit. Alas, he couldn't taste even one! The bunches were sold by Thomas, not giving any share to Selvan. Selvan's over-sincerity and honesty were very often criticised by the labourers. They considered him a simpleton.

The house under construction was two-storeyed, with an estimated value of over ten million rupees, and having all modern facilities. Thomas was a multi-millionaire landlord. But he was miserly in giving wages. The labourers who were sweating in the intolerable sunlight needed hot tea in the afternoon, and there were no teashops nearby. At other work sites, the house owners provided that. But Thomas did not do so, nor asked Selvan to bring it from the teashop.

Naturally the labourers disliked Thomas and I have heard them showering curses in his absence. They have complained to me about his inhuman treatment. Neither Thomas nor his wife ever spoke to these labourers or even asked their names. They very often spoke in praise of Dr. Martin who supplied them tea and snacks regularly at 4 p.m. when they worked at his site. I too started wondering why Thomas was so inconsiderate. Couldn't he ever think that these labourers were sweating their blood for this house, not for them to live in but only for him and his family? If their tears fell on the walls and floors, wouldn't that haunt him when he started living there? Had Thomas remembered what the great Malayalam poet, Vailoppally taught him at school, "Whenever I eat a grain of rice I can't but taste the tear of the farmer," he would have shown a little love and consideration to the labourers who sweated for the building. Fatigued by terrible heat, some of the labourers came for hot water to our house in the afternoon and my wife gave them tea. Just a compassionate act!

I now remember the selfless service Selvan had done for our neighbours. When the government supply of water failed for a few days, Selvan mae it his duty to supply water to these houses, pumping water from his master's well. How hastily he did it before Thomas arrived at the worksite! He had no doubt that his master would scold him if he knew of it.

Twice or thrice I had found Selvan's wife, Chellamma, at the work site. She had come to bring him back home. I too persuaded him to go with her. But his reply was that he would go home after two weeks. Selvan found much happiness in his work and stay here. Work was worship to him. He hated an idle life at his house even for a day.

~ ~ ~

"Selvan, stop crying. After all, that house is not yours, but the engineer's. When he asks you to get out, you have to. Face reality. You can't live there with the engineer and his family, can you? By the by, has he asked you to continue there as a security guard after today?"

"The engineer sir hasn't told me anything. As his daughter's marriage is next Sunday, I hope I will be staying there till then. I have many things to do here." His words were choked in his throat. It seemed that he had never anticipated a goodbye to the house, or he would not have been so much upset.

"OK, Selvan, go back to the engineer's house. I will be coming there shortly for dinner."

Selvan hesitantly returned. Within ten minutes, I followed with my wife and son for the house-warming dinner. I found Selvan standing desolate there at the corner of the front yard. We went to him directly and asked if he had anything to eat. He said no.

Many VIPs were coming and going. We too entered. We were welcomed by Thomas and his wife. We surveyed all the rooms of the house, which looked posh and luxurious. Then we took our food and got out. Selvan was still standing there like a stranger or even a beggar. Neither Thomas nor his wife cared a jot for him—not even cast their glance on him. We asked him to take the food and eat. He replied that he would do it later.

We came back to our house and observed what Selvan was doing. The labourers, who had been working throughout the night cleaning the premises, were assembled under the shade of a plastic sheet tied to a tree near the house. Selvan went to them, and along with them took a plate of fried rice from the kitchen and started eating sitting on the ground under the shade.

The dinner being over, Selvan and the labourers started cleaning the premises. Though he was working, his face was very gloomy. Thomas and his family spent their first night in the new house. Selvan might have slept in the garage. The next morning as I was reading the newspaper, Selvan came to me and announced in a low voice, "Sir, I am going back to my home."

"Aren't you staying till the marriage?"

"The engineer sir asked me to go back as my service was no more needed." There were tears in his eyes.

"Did the engineer give you anything extra?"

"I am yet to receive my salary, sir."

"Alright Selvan, go and stay with your wife and children. Spend your time with your grandchildren. They will entertain you."

"Thank you, sir. Thank you very much for the love shown towards me. Goodbye."

Selvan moved slowly to Mr. Thankappan's house, bade them goodbye and treaded towards Thomas's house. As it was time for me to go to college I could not see Selvan leaving our place.

The next day Salim, manager of my college canteen, completed Selvan's story from where I stopped. Selvan, straight from the engineer's house, went to Salim's hotel where he had been a customer for tea for the past one and a half years. Salim, a very kind man, gave him sufficient food with chicken curry as special. Neither did he charge for the food nor accepted the twenty rupees which Selvan tried to pay. Salim even offered him employment in his hotel for the daily wage of Rs. 150 in addition to free food and lodging. Selvan replied that he would consider it after consulting with his wife and children. Salim hired an auto rickshaw, paid its charge and sent Selvan to the bus stand.

"Salim, did the engineer give Selvan anything extra?"

"Only three hundred rupees, sir. How inconsiderate the man is! He could have given him at least a thousand rupees as extra. After all the poor man had worked for him day and night for the last one and a half years! Selvan's friends, with whom he used to drink the evening liquor, had asked him to sell the scrap iron rod pieces scattered on his master's work site and thus meet his expense. But he was such an honest man that he never did it. Such men are rare in this world."

"True, Salim. Honesty is never rewarded in this world. Had Mr. Thomas shown one percent of the love you have shown, Selvan could have gone to his house a happy man. The world has become so materialistic that love and kindness have no place here."

~ ~ ~

Commentary and Criticism

Review by Patricia Prime

Prof. K. V. Dominic is a poet, critic, short story writer and editor. *"Sanchita Karma" and Other Tales of Ethics and Choice from India* is his second collection of short stories. In his Preface to the book, Dominic says, "The themes include loneliness and problems of age, thirst for love, sexual desires, robbery and murder, terrorism, humanism..."

The book contains twenty stories. The opening title story, "Who is Responsible?" focuses on an elderly couple, Rehman and his wife Ramla. Sitting in his armchair watching the world go by, Rehman's mind drifts to his past. That's the beginning of the action, but not the beginning of the narrative. Dominic continues his theme with Rehman's son going overseas to work, leaving his wife behind and her relationship with another man. This leads to a violent murder.

Another of my favourites is "A Good Samaritan." Now, to be fair, I'm predisposed to like it because I recall the bible story I read years ago at school. Many people may have passed a road accident, but not many will have stopped to help. This is a sprightly and elegant story that takes a stock character and makes him and his story interesting through story and character construction. The Good Samaritan turns out to be the injured man who has aided many people in the past. I thought I knew exactly how the story would end—and then it didn't. It finished on an unexpected grace note.

The family saga of Joseph and Thomas in "Joseph's Maiden Vote for Parliament" is like having the company of friends who are trying to help each other with the tangle of politics. Thomas is a leading Advocate in the High Court, while his son Joseph is a B.Tech. student in the Govt. Engineering College at Kochi. Thomas' wife, Mercy is a professor in a government college and their daughter, Jane, is studying in a higher secondary school. The family tries to help Joseph make decisions about his politics but he has a mind of his own and the story ends with this firm decision:

"I don't want to cast my vote to any of these candidates. Where is the button for it?" Joseph exploded. "There is no button for it," getting from his seat, the presiding officer replied angrily.

'I don't want to vote for traitors," Joseph roared. "Political mafia Murdabad! Anna Hazare Zindabad! (Down with political mafia! Long live Anna Hazare) Political mafia Murdabad! Anna Hazare Zindabad!" Raising his right fist, Joseph thundered and ran out of the station. His slogan echoed from the neighbouring hills.

Crackling with imaginative flair, the author nails dialogue and our obsession with politics and politicians, while offering genuine insights into the character's thoughts and feelings.

In "Our Dear Bhai," the protagonist seems to hear the watchman of his college, Bhai, calling him. He says of him,

> Though he is illiterate, he can be sent as errant to any nook and corner of the country. During feats and celebrations in the college, he is at the forefront serving food and compelling us to eat more and more. He always has the adage that our happiness is his happiness.

An elegant ability with language and a strand of melancholia binds the short story, as the storyteller reveals that after Bhai passed, his wife did not receive his pension. He says,

> Why I heard Bhai calling me was only a hallucination, I understood. I returned to my house sad and forlorn.

The story, "The Twins," concerns a man who is always working on his computer whereas his wife feels very lonely, and so he adopts a stray cat. But, he says, "The very touch and cry of the cat removed my wife's solitude." Later, the cat, Sundari, gives birth to twin kittens but, when one kitten goes missing, a colleague gives them identical twin kittens, whom they name Manikutty and Amminikutty. After an accident with the twin kittens and the storyteller's mother, he decides to get rid of them. However, fate intervenes and he returns the kittens to his mother who has "experienced too much of solitude in my house that these kittens proved real companions" to her.

"World Environment Day" is the story of a thief, Kaatturaja, who is a "Six footed sturdy youth of thirty. He is ebony black with a twisted moustache on his ferocious face." This is a moral tale, with a twist to its end,

> As pledged and promised, Kaatturaja made a taskforce with his friends. The team of energetic twenty-odd youth started reforestation wherever barren strips were found. The forest rangers had little to do at all since Kaatturaja's team never allowed any trespassers to steal from the forest. After two years, the forest became a model to the world and the country nominated Kaatturaja and his team for the United Nations Forest for People Award.

This is a collection of stories evocative of the country with characters simply sketched in a few sentences while still feeling rounded and real. From the tentative beginnings of friendship, to family problems, running from life to finding fulfilment, pointed character studies and quiet meditations—Dominic's people are often bereft, put upon, always searching for something. Through them he speaks volumes in a short space about cause and effect in relationships.

~ ~ ~

Dr. Patricia Prime is an English poet, critic, reviewer, editor from New Zealand.

Review by Chandramoni Narayanaswamy

I have long been an avid reader of the poems of Dr. K. V. Dominic but had no occasion to read any of his short stories, though some have been published in journals as, stated by him in the preface. This bunch of twenty stories is his second venture in fiction and to put it briefly, is another testimonial to his literary genius. Though small in number, these deal with a wide spectrum of themes—the helplessness and loneliness of the aged, the thirst for love, crime and terrorism, religious intolerance and superstition, corruption and unemployment, the ever increasing divide between the haves and the have-nots, the exploitation of the poor by the rich, cruelty to animals, destruction of forests and environment, Christian spirit vis-à-vis Christian practice, cruel destiny and the helplessness of man, the need for multicultural harmony, the impact of mother tongue education, gender discrimination and empowerment of women etc. Like sips of cold water after a dusty walk in the hot sun, the vivid portrayal of these stark realities is relieved by instances of love, humanism, honesty, duty consciousness, compassion, repentance and reformation.

Dr. Dominic is both an idealist and a realist, one who sees things as they are, whose outlook is neither pessimistic nor optimistic but practical with the conviction that all is not lost. He is a Gandhian with firm adherence to ahimsa, a patriot and a secularist. Hence though a true Christian by birth and practice, he discards the theory generally believed in by majority of Christians that man is the supreme creation of God and He has given him the right to consume all other creatures; accepts what is rational in other religions and rejects what is irrational in his own. Hence he is a firm believer in the theory of karma and rebirth and is convinced that the reward of virtue and vice is to be reaped not in heaven and hell but on this earth through a series of births and rebirths. His love and compassion for animals and deep anguish at their suffering and the cruelty meted out to them, his honest indignation at the vices and evil practices we see around us, have found expression in his poems. His attempt to give vent to them through fiction is equally effective.

The story "Who is Responsible?" is thought-provoking, philosophical, and brain storming. Responsible for what? For a particular calamity or tragedy affecting an individual or a family or for catastrophes causing all-round havoc? For the degradation in values and the chaotic state of society in which God and conscience have no place? The story describes the pathetic life of a retired school teacher, a man of high character and integrity. His only son who could not come up to his expectations finds a job as an electrician in Oman, earns a lot of money, gets married at the instance of his parents to a rich and beautiful girl, and goes back to his job, leaving her with them. But instead of nursing the ailing mother-in-law, she moves around with her chauffeur, enjoying life, and finally elopes with him.

Simultaneously a letter comes informing the shocked father that his son had been arrested and dismissed from the job for his involvement in terrorist activities. The following day the old couple is found murdered and their house looted. There is no clue regarding the perpetrator. The author poses the question. Who is to be blamed for the tragedy of Rahman and his family? But more questions loom large before the readers. Did the daughter-in-law and her paramour have a hand in the crime? Did her infidelity provoke her husband to take to terrorism in his frustration? Was Rehman himself responsible for bringing about the tragedy by forcing his son to marry? The title poses a number of questions for which there is no answer.

In the story "Ammu's Birthday" in which a professor, having narrated the story of the misfortunes and tragedy of a family to his students, delivers a short lecture by way of replying to their comments and questions that mysterious are the ways of God, such miseries are part of the flow of the system and "as participatory beings we should flow with the system."

The "Good Samaritan" in the next story, having lost his only son in a road accident, had made it his life's mission to save other accident victims lying unattended on the road. He meets with the same fate and is saved by another good Samaritan. But his future is uncertain with the possibility of living through paralysis and loss of memory. This information is temporarily withheld from his doting wife, old parents and daughters but how long? Will Xavier miraculously regain normalcy? If not, what will the fate of his family? The reader is left to digest these questions.

"Best Government Servant" is also a story about good people who are ultimately rewarded and relieved of all their miseries in the end. As a story with a happy ending, it is refreshingly different from most stories we get to read these days, which end on a note of despair though some may feel it is too good to be true.

In sharp contrast to the old couple in the first story broken-hearted by the neglect and the humiliation meted out to them by their son and his wife is the old woman in "An E-mail from Senthil Kumar," tenderly taken care of by her overanxious son and daughter-in-law. She is a heart patient and they follow the doctor's advice that she should be spared all tension and sorrow to the letter by withholding all information about the calamities which befall her siblings, even to the extent of keeping her in the dark about the death of her youngest brother to whom she was deeply attached. She leads a happy life in blissful ignorance till like a bolt from the blue, the cat is let out of the bag by the son of the dead man who had come to invite them for his father's first death anniversary when she is alone in the house. Unable to bear the shock she suffers a severe stroke which she survives, only to lie in bed paralyzed and yearning for death. Objects of neglect and overprotection, all these the aged meet tragically.

Like spring following winter, the next story "Burn Your Horoscope!" is a happy one. A young man and woman hailing from orthodox Brahmin families remain single even after they are past their prime, though eligible in every respect, because the horoscopes of both predict death for the spouse within one year of marriage. They finally bring out matrimonial advertisements boldly revealing the dark prediction in their respective horoscopes. By a coincidence both the ads appear in the same paper on the same day and are read by both. Educated and rational in thinking, they decide to get married and, giving the lie to astrology and horoscopes, live long enough to celebrate their silver wedding. At the party thrown by their children to mark the occasion, the husband makes a speech in which he condemns astrology and exhorts his guests to throw their horoscopes in the fire.

"Joseph's Maiden Vote for Parliament" is a political satire. It vividly depicts the chaotic political situation in which avarice, hypocrisy and corruption reign supreme and the confusion and dilemma of young Joseph, who is to cast his vote for the first time in a parliamentary election racks his brain to decide to which party and which candidate he should give his vote to, but is unable to make his choice. He regards Anna Hazare as the messiah to usher in the new millennium. At the polling booth scanning the ballot paper with the names of the candidates and their symbols printed on it, his confusion reaches the climax and he nearly turns mad and rushes out of the booth shouting. "Political mafia murdabad! Anna Hazare Zindabad!" This would now evoke a smile from the reader who had seen how the euphoria generated by Anna Hazare ebbed out.

"Matthews, the Real Christian" and the "Twisted Course of Destiny" are sad commentaries on the state of unemployment and education in Kerala, where the percentage of literacy is the highest in India. In the second mentioned story, Rajiv and his sweetheart Sangeeta, both post-graduates, languish for years as teachers in private coaching centres getting meagre salaries. Sangeeta has better luck, because she belongs to a backward class and getting the benefit of reservation, secures appointment as a Lower Division Clerk in a government office and later as a Deputy Collector. Under parental pressure and persuaded by Rajiv, she is compelled to marry another.

Later Rajiv gets appointed as a peon in a Collectorate. Undaunted, he continues his research activities while working as a peon and is awarded a PhD. Destiny deals a cruel blow to him when Sangeeta is posted to the same office, and being a peon he has to carry files to her and take orders from her. She feels for him and prays for his luck. At last years of patient toil and perseverance are rewarded and Rajiv secures appointment as Assistant Professor in a govt. post graduate college. But the other story vividly highlights another stark and deplorable reality in addition to unemployment, namely the role of religion in politics and elections, making a mockery of democracy. Here, Matthews, as highly educated as Rajiv, having unsuccessfully knocked at the door of employment for any job, finally takes to self-employment for his livelihood and takes up agriculture on a small plot of two acres of land which he had inherited.

By dint of hard work, he becomes a successful agriculturist by combining cultivation with animal husbandry. He is an idealist, a socialist by conviction, loved and held in high esteem by all in the village. His popularity is sought to be exploited by politicians and much against his wishes, he is persuaded to contest the panchayat election as an independent candidate with the support of the left wing. He wins with a thumping majority and is elected as Panchayat President. As president, he is efficient, amiable and diplomatic and gets more funds for development of the panchayat, earning the respect and admiration of all including the opposition camp. At the same time he loses no opportunity to spread his own high principles and the message of secularism by exhorting religious leaders not to mix religion with politics.

Then comes the Assembly election and once again Matthews is persuaded to contest as an Independent with left wing support. His opponent, the candidate of the right wing, is also a catholic like him and has the full support of leaders of the three major religions—Islam, Hindu and Christianity who are alarmed at the prospect of victory of the secularist Matthews. Pastoral messages are published in papers and read in churches and seminaries pleading for votes to the right wing. There is high turnout in all booths and Matthew's victory is a foregone conclusion. But a few days before the declaration of the results, Matthews is killed in a hit and run road accident. His death is mourned by all, but his family is not allowed to enter the church to bury the body in the cemetery though they have a family tomb there for which they had paid money to the church.

Even though he was a true Christian who followed the teachings of Christ to the letter, the priest tells his brother that he was not a Christian as he never went to church and attended Mass. Finally bowing to public opinion, the gate of the cemetery is opened and the body is buried in the family tomb but without any prayers by the priest. No prayers were needed for the true Christian.

This story makes one look back and take a peep into history when in the late fifties the first Communist government in Kerala was democratically elected in a fair and free election; an event which made the capitalist western block led by America feel glittery and threatened and an efficient, corruption-free government was dismissed by the central government on the ground of irretrievable breakdown of law and order, which was brought about by the direct involvement of the church, the provocation being the move to nationalize education by taking over all private schools and colleges, the majority of which were under the church. Other religious organizations like the NSS and the Muslim League too had joined the agitation. The rot which had set in Kerala politics then had now grown into a mafia and spread to many other States in the country.

There is an air of mystery and supernatural in "Our Dear Bhai" and "Sanchita Karma." In the first story, the Gurkha watchman of a college, who had grown grey in the service of the institution, devoting himself to the care of its staff and students made it all his world and wanted to continue there in some capacity even after retirement, dies of sudden cardiac arrest while still in service. He is greatly missed and he seems to speak to a teacher who loved him through the rustling of the leaves of a mango tree which he had planted and nurtured to perpetuate his memory in the college.

In "Sanchita Karma," seven cats, pampered and brought up with loving care by their owners in their previous births had been poisoned to death by their affluent and snobbish neighbours, an advocate and his wife, take revenge on their murderers who have been reborn as two mice by chasing them for a long time. When questioned why they are so cruel to them, they narrate the story of their previous births. They were three generations of cats who used to trespass into the property of the advocate and though they never ventured into the house or stole any food, they would defecate in the compound, which could not be tolerated by the wealthy couple who were ostensibly pious Christians who went to church every day and regularly attended Mass.

In this story, the matriarch of the cat family becomes the mouthpiece of the author. Like Bernard Shaw, he gives vent through her views on cruelty to animals, his total rejection of the philosophy that man is supreme among God's creations and all other forms of life are meant for his enjoyment and benefit and his firm belief in karma and rebirth. The story is also autobiographical. The merciless elimination of the cats by neighbours is an episode from his own life and the death of the cats is the subject of one of his tear jerking poems "Ammini's Laments" included in his second anthology *Write Son, Write*. Ammini is the name of one of the seven cats in this story.

"The Twins" is also a story about cats with an autobiographical touch. Two cats named Manikkutty and Amminikkutty (names of two of the seven cats in "Sanchita Karma") are the darling pets of a college teacher and a school teacher like the author and his wife. The cats lead a blissful life till their master's mother comes to stay with them. She is a heart patient and the master is worried about the disturbance and tension that would be caused to her by the kittens who have the free run of the house. His fears are proved right when the old lady is alone in the house after he and his wife had left for college and school and he comes at lunch time to find his mother lying helpless on the bed gasping for breath, the kittens having knocked down her food and medicines from a table.

Having revived her with emergency medicines, the master of the kittens takes a hard decision to abandon them for his mother's sake. With a heavy heart he takes the kittens in a carton, drives to a lonely place and leaves them there. But when he is about to return from that place, he gets a phone call from his mother about the missing kittens and insisting on their being brought back. The kittens are taken back and a home nurse is engaged to look after the old lady and all are happy.

"School Entrance Festival" depicts a tragi-comic situation where education in government and government-aided schools goes a begging. A school which was once a model for other schools and used to have a strength of 1500 students and more than sixty teachers is reduced to a state of imminent extinction with only fifty students in ten standards and fifteen teachers. Before reopening, the manager calls a meeting and informs the teachers that there was not a single child for admission in the first standard, for which they could somehow get one student in the previous year. If they fail to get at least one pupil that year standard-I will be abolished, paving the way for closure of the school. So the teachers go in search of a pupil and finally manage to secure a five-year old girl, Vidya, daughter of a casual labourer in a slum by wooing her widowed mother with incentives like monthly payment of Rs. 10,000/- for the family to meet their expenses, three sets of uniforms, a school bag and an umbrella for the child.

Having conceded all the demands of the family living in poverty (who had been approached earlier by teachers of government L P Schools with offers of uniforms, bag and umbrella), they make advance payment of Rs.10,000 and give a packet of sweets to the child to ensure her being brought to the school on reopening day. On that day, the school is decorated as for a festival and the child is received like a VIP with bouquets and toys while flower petals are showered on her. The child looks for friends but there is no one on that day or afterwards. For the whole year, Vidya studies in Standard-I with the teacher as her only companion. This is the situation prevailing in other classes, too.

Such a situation has been brought about by the mad rush for admission in English medium CBSE schools, to which the teachers in government and government-aided L P Schools also send their children in preference to their own schools. The story was like a fairytale to me, who had studied in Malayalam medium in the Government Girls High School at Alleppey in Kerala in the early fifties (English medium had been abolished from schools after independence and there were no English medium schools then).

"Selvan's House" vividly presents the merciless exploitation of labour by the rich. A wealthy engineer is constructing a palatial house and he is so miserly that he does not provide even a cup of tea in the afternoon to the construction workers toiling in the hot sun, who are often given food and tea by kinder neighbours. Selvan, who supervises the construction, is simple and hardworking, so devoted to his work as if he is constructing his own house and has almost started regarding it as his own as it nears completion. But once the work is over, he is discarded like a soiled glove and dismissed curtly by the engineer and his wife, who move into the house immediately after the housewarming party. It is difficult to believe that such exploitation of labour is possible in Kerala, which is regarded as the birthplace of communism in India.

There is an element of mysticism in the story "World Environment Day," in which trees and animals, as symbols of long exploited nature, interact with man to bring about a miraculous change in the wanton destruction of forests. Katturaja, meaning king of the forest, is the illegitimate son of a tribal woman conceived after she was raped by forest guards. Despised by all, he grows up thirsting for revenge, and after getting some education, he learns how the tribals are cheated and exploited by government officials and forest mafia. To take revenge and alleviate the distress of tribals, he takes to crime himself and becomes a sort of Robin Hood by felling trees like sandal, teak and mahogany, selling the valuable timber to the agents of timber merchants, and distributing the money among the poor. He is the most wanted forest thief.

On World Environment Day, when he is about to fell a teak tree, the tree cries for help which is heard by a herd of tuskers who rush to its rescue. Terrified at their approach, Katturaja scrambles up the tree and is trapped on a high branch unable to come down as the tuskers have surrounded the tree, ready to attack him if he comes down. In that helpless situation, he is able to hear the voice of the tree, which tries to reason with him. He has a change of heart, seeks the forgiveness of the tree and promises to be the friend and protector of the forest to atone for his past life as the destroyer. The elephants in turn understand his language and retreat. Katturaja comes down, a reformed man, surrenders before the Magistrate and voluntarily courts arrest. He faces trial for his past crimes and is sentenced to imprisonment and released on the next World Environment Day.

On his return, he is welcomed by all inhabitants of the forest birds, animals and trees. He forms a voluntary action force of youths to protect the forest, and in two years it becomes a model forest with Katturaja and his team being nominated for the United Nation's "Forest For People" award. The story also conveys a message that the observance of World Environment Day should not be limited to making speeches from the platform but should be observed by doing something tangible to preserve and protect forests and environment and the flora and fauna.

The stories in this collection not only storm the brain, but also delight the heart and will be treasured by all lovers of contemporary Indo-English fiction. It is hoped that more such stories will flow from the pen of Dr. Dominic in quick succession.

~ ~ ~

Chandramoni Narayanaswamy is an English poet, short story writer, novelist, essayist and translator. He is a retired Indian Administrative Service (IAS) Officer from Bhubaneswar, Odisha, India.

Review by Radhamani Sarma

I am delighted to review the book of short stories by Prof. K. V. Dominic. An academician of diligence and skill, poet and ebullient critic, he needs no introduction. He is a prolific writer who touches almost all aspects of Indian life. There can be no better and fitting assessment than his own avowed approach to his writing corpus. Themes such as old age, loneliness, corruption, pitfalls of human foibles etc., are inherent in his imagination taking shape to reach the public in good earnest. The story "Who is Responsible?" focuses on multiple themes such as separation between a couple, especially newlyweds, that might result in elopement, political pitfalls, murder for gain, etc.

In almost all his short stories, the locale is his favourite Kerala. Diction dipped in practical observation of forthrightness, the story is about the protagonist's son, and daughter-in-law Aisha, who deviates from ethics in the absence of her husband when he takes a job abroad. The storyteller observes in his own candid way, "She was young, healthy and full of passion. It was true, she was a bride, but her body knew no ethics. Who would satiate her carnal needs?" "Misfortunes never strike singly" is proved, when towards the end of the story, Rehman and his wife were murdered for gain, the writer wailing that poetic justice is missing. Innocents are done with. Verily true.

In the story, "A Good Samaritan," the writer himself begins stating that it is three fourth real and rest based on fantasy. Kerala pops out of his imagining, stamping its rightful place. The persona narrating the story of Xavier, a Good Samaritan who saved so many accident victims, is the accident victim now, facing loss of memory. Xavier and his wife lost their only son in an accident. God's ways are mysterious, we do not know. Those who were saved by him now are saddened by the fact that he is in trauma. We all go by the time-honoured dictum declared in the Torah: "Charity will stand by us forever" (Iggeret HaKodesh, end of Epistle 4).

"The Best Government Servant" is one, like Krishnan, who has principles not to accept bribes. In a corruption-rampant society bribery is a canker. Either you are rewarded or punished for being honest. In a native immediacy of tone and feeling, the story is carried on. "Ammu's Birthday" is another depiction wherein God's ways sometimes appear cruel. In the close of Ammu's birthday celebrations, (fatherless child) she has a tragic end much to the plight of her mother, a widow; what to call this? A philosophy often prevails in our lives, God's ways are mysterious and we all need to believe and go with the flow of life, be it filled with setbacks and twists and turns. Yet another story reveals that a weak heart cannot take bad or sad news. Mother, memories and medicines which sustain her all through—a weak heart—"An Email Message from Senthilkumar" means a lot. Candid recordating of human dilemma, bonds and bondages in our lives—all can be visualised. Nowadays, horoscopes play a vital role in our matrimonial market and at the same time prove to be futile before human foresight. "Burn Your Horoscope", humorously coiled by wisdom on either side of bride and bridegroom fructifies marriage and prosperity.

The prolific writer's potential is testified by a simple yet realistic depiction of various characters drawn from all walks of life. The poet-short story writer portrays characters in such a way that the words emphatically flow from their mouths—stay in our minds—as if they are time bound and dictums for all ages. For instance, in "Matthews, the Real Christian," Matthews says, "I request your religious leaders not to mix religion with politics. Let religion go its way and politics its way. Hasn't Christ taught us, "Give unto Caesar, Caesar's and unto God God's?" You should not request laymen to vote for this party or that man... It is high time we stop discrimination to women. Being the children of God there is no discrimination between man and woman. Then why should they be denied entry in God's abode?"

Not only society is of concern for Dominic, even tenets of philosophy, Hindu philosophy, take roots in the writer's short stories. Karma theory is unfolded, in the story "Sanchita Karma" emphasising related aspects such as rebirth and God's will in re-creation. The story via conversation between cats and male mouse and female mouse, is Karma theory and rebirth enumerated. Our lives veer round our affinity between people with whom we live, interact and spend. Bhai in the story "Our Dear Bhai" is a Gurkha, a watchman in the college, a lovely character whose day to day involvement is worth mentioning. "World Environment Day" is a story in which the preservation of forests is very vital in our lives and Katturaja the forest thief, after reformation and before his interaction with elephants and trees reveals much. The book is alive in pages--interesting episodes, witty and lively dialogue.

~ ~ ~

Dr. Radhamony Sarma is a retired Professor of English, English language poet and a critic from Chennai, India.

Review by Sulakshna Sharma

K. V. Dominic's book, *"Sanchita Karma" and Other Tales of Ethics and Choice from India* is his second collection of twenty short stories. Many of these, according to the author, "have been published periodically through... [his] own edited journals as well as through other international refereed journals, both print and online" (Preface). Dominic has "used several themes and focused on many issues, which are universal and at the same time frequently occurring in... [his] own State, Kerala" (Preface). The themes are mainly socio-political and socio-economic. The tone is satirical and, at times, didactic.

The author has enlisted a number of themes in the preface to his book on which his stories are based. Succinctly, the various themes can be put under the following main headings: unemployment, Diaspora and its repercussions, devaluation and the frustration of highly educated youth in a highly literate State like Kerala; superstitions, immorality and modernity, discrimination on the basis of caste and social status, the follies in the Indian marriage system, communism versus democracy, corruption and political exploitation of the weak and the downtrodden, plight of the poor, wildlife and its conservation, the Hindu religious philosophy of karma, et cetera.

The characters and their social milieu are plausible and interesting. Every story brings into light a bunch of fresh problems, and themes are explored and realized by its characters to the fullest. Every story leaves a stinging question that forces its reader to rethink his/her role and contribution toward society. For example, at the end of his short story, "Ammu's Birthday," an English Professor, Dr. Sankar, asks his class about the story he had just read for them. The students, referring to the story as an ordinary one, insisted that they wanted "to hear something merry and pleasant" as "tragic incidents" are rife in newspapers. Perturbed by such responses, Dr. Sankar tries to explain the need of such a "tragic" story, thus:

My dear students, I honour your reactions. What Joseph said is true. This is just an ordinary story. I am not revealing the author's name. And what relevance has an author in a work as per New Criticism? The author has mentioned as a footnote that the story is based on a tragedy at a village in North Kerala. As Meera has complained, we are reading such tragic lives every day. Dear students, don't forget the fact that our sweetest songs are those that tell of saddest thoughts, as Shelley has written. The more we read such things, the more compassionate and humane we should become. Such literature purges our mind and we get karunyam (compassion) rasa. We should not turn our faces to miseries and tragedies of others. Such tragedies are part of the flow of the system and as participatory beings we should flow with the system. Mysterious are the ways of the Creator and our little intelligence can't find justifications for the multitudinous activities of the Almighty. Hope you are satisfied with my answers." Dr. Sankar ended his lecture.

Clearly, the aim of the author as a "social critic" has always been the betterment of his society, State and nation.

Most of the stories have a sombre tone. They exhibit various socio-political-economic vignettes and are brimming with moral implications: "Who is Responsible?" "A Good Samaritan," "Best Government Servant," "Ammu's Birthday," "An Email from Senthil Kumar," "Joseph's Maiden Vote for Parliament," "Matthews, the Real Christian," "Our Dear Bhai," "Sanchita Karma," "Selvan's House," "Twisted Course of Destiny," and "Is Human Life Precious than Animal's?" all do. In comparison to the above mentioned short stories, the following stories put forward the message of the significance of rational thinking, morality, compassion and humanity in a more jovial and a light-hearted manner: "Burn Your Horoscope!" "School Entrance Festival," "The Twins," "World Environment Day," and "Puppets in the Hands of God."

In conclusion, the book is a true mirror of the society that writhes under the burden of economic insecurities and lack of good governance. Most of the stories in the book can be adapted for small plays, skits, and even TV serials—aiming to spread social awareness on the burning issues and rampant evils in the Indian society and the Indian political system. Moreover, the stories can be easily incorporated in English textbooks of any school or college. Its copies in the school and college libraries will contribute toward nurturing the young minds of India and making them more humane, considerate and socially aware citizens. I congratulate K. V. Dominic for the success of his noble pursuit.

~ ~ ~

Dr. Sulakshna Sharma is an Associate Professor of English, critic, and editor from Himachal Pradesh, India.

About the Author

Dr. K. V. Dominic, English poet, critic, short story writer and editor is a retired professor of the Post Graduate & Research Department of English, Newman College, Thodupuzha, Kerala, India. He was born on 13 February 1956 at Kalady, a holy place in Kerala where Adi Sankara, the philosopher who consolidated the doctrine of Advaita Vedanta was born. He took his PhD on the topic "East-West Conflicts in the Novels of R. K. Narayan with Special Reference to *The Vendor of Sweets, Waiting for the Mahatma, The Painter of Signs* and *The Guide*" from Mahatma Gandhi University, Kottayam, Kerala.

In addition to innumerable poems, short stories and critical articles published in national and international journals, he has authored/edited thirty-five books so far, including six poetry books in English, one each translated into Hindi and Gujarati. *Sanchita Karma and Other Tales of Ethics and Choice from India* is his second collection of stores. Some of the stories of this book were originally published in his first short story collection *Who is Responsible?* published by Authorspress, New Delhi in 2016.

Prof. Dominic is the Secretary of Guild of Indian English Writers, Editors and Critics (GIEWEC), a non-profit registered organisation having now 250 members mainly consisting of university/college professors, research scholars and professional English writers. He is the Editor and Publisher of the international refereed biannual journal in English, *International Journal on Multicultural Literature* (IJML), and Editor-in-Chief of the Guild's international refereed biannual journal, *Writers Editors Critics* (WEC).

Four books on his poetry—both poetry and criticism—were published from the same publishing house, Modern History Press, in 2016 and 2017. International Poets Academy, Chennai conferred on him its highest award Lifetime Achievement Award in 2009. India Inter-Continental Cultural Association, Chandigarh conferred on him Kafla Inter-continental Award of Honour Sahitya Shiromani in recognition of his contribution in the field of literature in 2014. Dr. Dominic can be contacted at: prof.kvdominic@gmail.com Website: www.profkvdominic.com.

Goa Outreach:
Helping Street and Slum Children in India

Goa Outreach is a small project helping local disadvantaged children regardless of their religion, class, caste or gender. Many of these children are slum and street children who have arrived in Goa alone or with their families from neighbouring states in the hope of an easier and better life. Many children end up working on the streets to support the family income, this is often in the form of rag  picking with children, usually in small groups, walking around the streets picking up items which are later sold at recycling centres. Other children can be found working the beaches begging, selling trinkets or other small items.

Goa Outreach provides a route into full-time education by accessing schools for the children and providing support to encourage them to stay in school on a regular basis. The support includes uniforms, books, bags, footwear, fees and other requirements and of course keeping a check on their performance and attendance.

Health is another important role as the children we help often suffer from long-term health problems, treatment for which is not always available early on and slum conditions may well exacerbate these problems. Scabies, impetigo, conjunctivitis are common issues that are easily spread with burns and infected mosquito bites often going untreated resulting in more severe infections leaving scars as well as the danger of contracting Malaria or Dengue Fever.

To help the children with health care we provide free medicines and pay for any hospital or doctors fees. In addition to this, we also give out monthly health packs to promote cleanliness. Mosquito protection is also given to families as Malaria, and other vector borne diseases are a threat to families living in the slums.

We want to be able to give street and slum children a chance of a childhood worth remembering. We want them to study hard, but we also want to provide them with a safe and fun environment with access to toys and games which other children take for granted.

With this in mind, we created Goa Outreach. Please check out our blogs which are updated monthly.

www.GoaOutreach.org

K. V. Dominic Essential Readings gathers for the first time the three most important works of poetry from this shining new light of contemporary Indian verse in English: *Winged Reason, Write Son, Write* and *Multicultural Symphony*. A fourth collection of 22 previously unpublished poems round out a complete look at the first 12 years of Dominic's prolific and profound verse. Each poem includes unique Study Guide questions suitable for South Asian studies curricula.

Written in free verse, each of his poems makes the reader contemplate on intellectual, philosophical, spiritual, political, and social issues of the present world. Themes range from multiculturalism, environmental issues, social mafia, caste-ism, exploitation of women and children, poverty, and corruption to purely introspective matters. From the observation of neighbourhood life to international events, and everyday forgotten tragedies of India, nothing escapes the grasp of Dominic's keen sense of the fragility of life and morality in the modern world.

~ ~ ~

"K. V. Dominic is one of the most vibrant Indian English poets whose intense passion for the burning social and national ailments makes him a disciple of Ezekielean School of poetry. His poetic passion for the natural beauty keeps him besides the Romanticists."

—Dr. A. K. Choudhary, English poet, critic and editor, Professor of English, Assam, India

K.V. Dominic Essential Readings: Poems about Social Justice, Women's Rights, and the Environment (ISBN 978-1-61599-302-4)